"Chris and Andie, Sitting in a Tree, K-I-S-S-I-N-G"

Chris slid back across the seat and closed the car door. "I think we ought to teach those brats a lesson."

Suddenly he bent his head close to mine and kissed me on the lips. I felt his fingers pressing cool at the back of my neck and the most amazing sense of peace filtered through me.

I was vaguely conscious of shrieks and of small bodies flailing against the car. Chris looked around momentarily to check our audience and then smiled and kissed me again.

When he finally drew away from me, I shook my hair back in place and took a few deep breaths. "Is this part of some grand plan of yours or something?" I asked uneasily. "I mean is there some particular reason you're kissing me like that?"

"Sure. My idea is that if we kiss like this every time we pull up in front of the house, eventually they'll get bored with the whole thing. Right?"

I looked around me at the little faces pressing their noses against the car windows. "I wouldn't hold my breath," I said.

Books by Janice Harrell

Andie and the Boys
Dooley Mackenzie Is Totally Weird
Brace Yourself, P.J.

Wild Times at West Mount High
Easy Answers
Senior Year at Last

Available from ARCHWAY Paperbacks

Brace Yourself, P.J.

Janice Harrell

AN ARCHWAY PAPERBACK
Published by POCKET BOOKS

New York   London   Toronto   Sydney   Tokyo   Singapore

AN ARCHWAY PAPERBACK *Original*

An Archway Paperback published by
POCKET BOOKS, a division of Simon & Schuster
1230 Avenue of the Americas, New York, NY 10020

ISBN: 0-671-69670-X

First Archway Paperback printing April 1991

10 9 8 7 6 5 4 3 2 1

AN ARCHWAY PAPERBACK and colophon are registered trademarks of Simon & Schuster.

Cover art by Mort Engel, Photographer

Printed in the U.S.A.

IL 6+

Brace Yourself,

P.J.

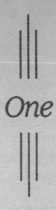

One

Everyone knew that no meaningful social life occurred at school-sponsored functions—everyone but my mother.

"Why aren't they going to have a spring dance at school?" she asked me.

"Because nobody would go."

"That's ridiculous, Andie. Why not?"

"Because it wouldn't be cool, that's why."

I knew all about cool through my stepbrother, P.J., and his friends Dooley MacKenzie and Chris Hamilton. Being cool was their profession. I worried too much and studied too hard to be cool, but I did get a certain amount of reflected glory just being around P.J. and his friends.

"What about that lovely dance you went to in the fall?" Mom asked. "You had a wonderful time. I wish they'd do something like that again."

Mom had a weak spot for dances. A novelist by trade, she seemed to think all dances were magnets for mysterious dark strangers and beautiful women with secret pasts. Nobody could ever accuse her of being a realist. But why, I wondered, was she suddenly harping on the subject? I was beginning to think something was behind her questions.

"Mom, are you thinking I'm miserable about breaking up with Pete? Because I'm not. I'm really enjoying my freedom."

"That's wonderful, darling," she said doubtfully. "I'm glad. Really."

P.J. burst in through the kitchen door just then with Chris and Dooley right behind him. Mom recoiled before the advance of so many sweaty male bodies. "There's more tropical punch in the pantry, boys," she told them, "if you run out."

"Thanks, Mrs. Grouman." Chris stepped in the door. He was close to six feet with tousled blond hair and eyes of periwinkle blue. Chris was the most devastatingly attractive of my stepbrother's friends. But since I'd gotten to know him, I almost forgot about how good he looked most of the time. He was just Chris who hung out at our house in clothes that were not only sweaty, but sometimes positively ripe.

"I stopped by the bakery too," Mom went on. "There are éclairs on top of the fridge."

P.J. fixed the white bags on the fridge with the narrow-eyed gaze of a predator. It was amazing to me how he managed to stay so skinny, the way he ate.

Mom smiled vaguely, then with a wave of her hand floated out of the room and back to her study to write.

Although I look like my mom—we both have slight builds and masses of auburn hair—I am not the sort who floats. I am forthright and practical. Another difference between us was that I didn't think that some enchanted evening my prince would show up at a school-sponsored dance. In fact, I didn't even want one to. At this time in my life my major ambition in the romance field was to be a free agent. When I was going with Pete Joyner, I had gotten totally sick of being "Pete's girlfriend." The whole experience reminded me of something I had heard a friend say once. "When you go with a guy, it's like you two become one. But the one is him." New Year's Eve I had made a major resolution—never again.

"Éclairs," said P.J., tearing open a bag. "Aw-right!"

Dooley collapsed onto a kitchen chair. "Get me something to drink. I'm about ready to pass out."

"Get it yourself!" said P.J.

Dooley stumbled to the sink, groped for a tumbler, and ran water into it. His ocher-colored hair had tumbled onto his forehead, and the back of his shirt was stained with sweat.

It was obvious the guys had been doing something strenuous, but I was vague about what it was. Sandlot baseball, shooting baskets, and tennis all blurred together in my mind. When a ball was flying through the air, my only concern was that it not land on my head.

"Who won?" I asked.

"Nobody. We were just throwing a Frisbee around."

I studied the sweaty smudge P.J.'s arm had left on the kitchen counter. "You were just playing Frisbee?" I repeated. "Then how come you're all wiped out?"

Chris shrugged. "Well, we did play touch football with some guys at the park first."

P.J. upended a tumbler filled with tropical punch, swallowed, and then wiped his mouth with the back of his hand. "We finally had to quit. All these little girls were clumped around the goal, staring at Chris. We were afraid we'd trample them."

Chris laughed. "My groupies."

"Too bad they were only in fifth grade, Chris."

"I can wait," said Chris.

P.J. tossed a doughnut hole in the air, and Chris caught it with one hand.

"Then we ran all the way home," Dooley explained. "Boy, do I need to get back in shape. I got awful soft this winter." He pounded on his flat stomach with his fist.

"We saw Pete over at the park," said P.J. "He fixed those hound dog eyes on us, and I was afraid he was going to say, 'Take a message to Andie for me' or something gross like that. So we got out of there fast."

"You're making that up, P.J.," I said.

"No, honest. He was there. Tell her, Dooley."

"Stop it, you guys," said Chris. "Leave Andie alone.

4

She had the sense to cut loose from Pete, and that's *good,* man, so shut your mouths."

"Anyway," I said. "It wouldn't mean anything to me at all. Pete and I are just friends now."

For some reason they all seemed to find this very funny.

"Okay, laugh," I said crossly. "But it happens to be true."

"We believe you," said P.J. "We believe you." He slid down into the kitchen chair and considered his éclair thoughtfully. "I wonder if Brian's going to have to get stitches," he said.

"Nah," said Dooley. "Sure, he was bleeding a lot. But it wasn't that big a deal."

I quelled a shudder. What the guys considered fun never ceased to amaze me. If a bunch of girls went out on a muddy field and banged their heads together until one of them had to go to the hospital for stitches, people would think they were crazy. But when boys do it, they call it sport.

"If Brian didn't have bad luck," said P.J., "he wouldn't have any luck at all. He got hit with a driving-under-the-influence charge after Harry Litchfield's party last weekend. He was so loaded that he forgot to leave his car there and walk. He climbed in and started to drive off. He wasn't even halfway down the street before they nailed him. They stopped me, too, but I was dead sober." He laughed. "My mamma didn't raise no idiots."

"I think that was the night I took Rachel to a

movie," said Dooley. He chomped into a doughnut. Dooley went with my best friend, Rachel Green. I had never quite understood their relationship, but it suited them fine.

"I guess I missed the cops," said Chris. "I left early because I had to get up the next morning."

"Maybe I ought to go to one of these parties," I said. "Just to see what they're like."

"You'd hate it," said Chris.

"I promise you," said P.J. "Just a bunch of people standing around talking. Dull."

"If it's so dull, why do you guys keep going to them?"

P.J. shrugged. "Have to get out and see people, don't we?"

I cast a glance over my shoulder, but I didn't see Mom creeping up to eavesdrop. I was glad because I didn't think P.J.'s picture of the real social life of Westmarket High would reassure her.

Not that everybody at Westmarket High went to wild parties. I didn't, for instance. But P.J. ran in more exciting circles than I did. He was cool.

I was always faintly surprised that P.J. managed to keep Mom and Richard from knowing exactly how exciting his social life was. I think that he was so uncommunicative with them that they gave up asking him questions. They must have figured as long as he didn't call from jail, things were okay.

"Get this, guys," said Chris. "My mom said I could have a party."

We all turned to stare at him. Even I knew that wild parties were usually held when kids' parents were out of town.

"So anyway," Chris said, slathering jam on a slice of bread, "my mom said fine, have a party. But you've got to send out invitations, and we'll hire a cop to stand at the gate checking to make sure nobody comes that isn't invited."

Dooley guffawed. "So what'd you say?"

"What do you think I said? No, thanks. I said that's not what I call a party."

"Parents," said Dooley disdainfully. Ever since Dooley's father had remarried and changed the easy-going bachelor habits of their household, Dooley had been very down on families.

"Brian flunked his algebra final too," P.J. said suddenly. "And that's on top of getting charged."

Chris shoved him. "Don't keep *thinking* about it, man. It's not your problem. Don't let it get to you."

"It's not getting to me. I was just thinking about luck. You know I got a B on that algebra exam."

"That's not luck," said Chris with feeling. "That's a miracle."

"I know, I know." P.J.'s fingers were drumming on the countertop. "But what I figure it shows is that luck is running my way. I have a real strong feeling about that. After that B was posted, I started thinking nothing could go wrong. This could be it—my *year*, man."

"Why not?" Chris propped his feet up on a chair, and a toe poked out of his ancient tennis shoe.

"It's just that after Suzy dumped me, I got this kind of feeling that maybe I was doomed."

"That was before New Year's," Chris pointed out. "That doesn't affect your luck this year. Every year is a fresh start."

"You're right," P.J. said. "In fact, what I've been thinking is this—I might just be on a roll."

"Go with that," said Chris.

"I just want to think of some way to use this good luck before it runs out, that's all."

Right about then I had a faint stirring of anxiety. "What exactly do you have in mind?" I asked.

"I'm not sure." P.J.'s eyes took on a distant look. "But it should be something really neat."

"Have a party!" put in Dooley.

"Sure. Right, Dooley," said P.J.

"It stands to reason your folks have to go away sometime," said Dooley.

"They're going away next week," said P.J. "But a lot of good it does me."

"They're going on a Caribbean cruise," I explained. "They didn't have much time for a honeymoon last summer, so this is supposed to make up for it."

"Hey, Dooley is right, man!" said Chris. "You could have a party."

P.J. made a face. "No such luck. Great-aunt Millie is coming to stay with us. Is that grim or what?"

"Is there something about Great-aunt Millie that I

8

ought to know?" I shot him an uneasy glance. Great-aunt Millie was my stepfather Richard's aunt, and though I knew she was coming to stay with us, I had never met the lady.

"Nah. She's just your average old lady who dyes her hair red and wears Reeboks. But she's not going to let us have a party, I can tell you."

Although I didn't say it out loud, I was relieved to hear it.

"Don't worry," Chris told P.J. "If you're really on a lucky streak, you'll have lots of chances to use it."

"Yeah." P.J. gave a little laugh. "Maybe I'll ask Maggie Parker to go out with me."

"You ought to do that," said Chris. "She's a nice girl. I bet you two would get along."

P.J. tried ineffectually to smooth his cowlick. "Honest to God, Chris, nobody but Dooley and me would put up with you. Would they, Dooley? I mean you're a guy who's road tested half the girls in school."

"Maggie and me were just good friends," said Chris.

"Right. Sure."

Chris had the kind of reputation that made it impossible for people to believe he was just friends with any girl. That had been one of Pete's complaints. He didn't like me to be friendly with Chris because people talked, he said. Pete was awfully sensitive about things like that. It was one of the things about him that had just about driven me out of my mind.

I surveyed the guys over my cola, letting the fizz

tickle my nose. I couldn't pretend I actually understood them. I wasn't sure why they loved big noisy parties or why they were so crazy about working out and running around in the cold and the mud, but I had gotten used to them. I was so used to them I could practically predict what they were going to say. There was something nice about that.

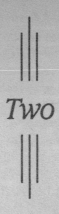

Two

"I can't believe it!" Mom was poring over the letter she had just opened. "Great-aunt Millie has come down with the mumps."

Richard walked into the kitchen, adjusting his tie. "That's ridiculous. Who ever heard of a sixty-seven-year-old woman having the mumps? You must have it wrong." He snatched the letter from her hand and glared at it. "The mumps! How can she have the mumps?"

"I knew we should have taken out trip insurance," groaned Mom. "What do you bet the cruise company won't give us any refund at all?"

Richard gave his tie a sharp tug. "Listen, Ellen, we aren't going to need a refund," he said grimly. "We're going on that cruise."

"But we can't just leave the kids here to fend for themselves for an entire week."

P.J. and I exchanged startled glances.

"I don't see why not. They're not three-year-olds."

Mom shook her head. "I don't know, Richard."

P.J. knew better than to make his father suspicious by acting pleased at this turn of events. His face was carefully expressionless.

"What do you think, kids?" asked Richard. "Can you get along on your own for a week?"

P.J. shrugged. "No problem."

"But Andie's never been left by herself," protested Mom. "I'm not sure I feel right about it."

"She won't be by herself," Richard pointed out. "P.J. will be here. And we can have Jerry and Sue look in on the kids, if you want."

"We'll be fine, Mom," I said.

P.J. shot me a grateful look. Actually, I was not at all sure we would be fine. But I knew what P.J. expected me to say.

"It's stupid for us to sit around here when we've already paid for the cruise," argued Richard.

"I guess you're right." Mom still looked very uncertain.

Richard turned a stern eye on us. "Of course, we expect you kids to keep to the rules just as if we were here. No skipping school. No staying up late on school nights."

He didn't say "no wild parties," but I for one felt that was implicit in the instructions.

"Yes, sir," said P.J.

I carefully avoided looking at P.J. when Richard started going on about how lucky he and Mom were to have kids they could trust. What I was thinking was that I was witnessing an interesting psychological phenomenon. Richard had never trusted P.J. before. In fact, he always seemed to suspect that P.J. was up to no good. But now that he had a paid-in-full Caribbean vacation at stake, he was suddenly sure that P.J. was mature and responsible.

"All right, it's settled, then," Richard said. "We'll give you kids a call midway through the week just to see how things are going."

"But, Richard, we're going to be out on a boat."

"They have phones, El. I promise you, they have phones."

I could hear Mom and Richard still arguing as they went upstairs. I could imagine what Mom was saying. She is not a worrier by nature, but once she starts, she goes wild. I guess it's because she has such a powerful imagination. She was probably pointing out that in their absence the earthquake of the century could strike or that P.J. and I might be captured by extraterrestrials. What I felt reasonably sure of was that she was not prophesying that we would have a wild party. Mom still believed that every student at Westmarket High was sitting around waiting for the big excitement of a school-sponsored dance.

"Hey," said P.J., darting a swift glance at me. "How about that, huh? They're leaving us here by ourselves."

I stood up. "Remember, P.J., we're supposed to abide by all the rules when they're gone."

"Sure." He rubbed his hands together. "But what they don't know won't hurt them, right?"

I swallowed hard. It was extremely important that I be on good terms with P.J. I mean, I had to live with him. I sensed it would not be wise for me to follow my instincts and run upstairs screaming, "Don't leave me! Don't leave me!" So I didn't. But I felt like it.

Mom and Richard left early Tuesday morning.

"Bon voyage!" we called as they pulled their car onto the street.

"Remember, kids!" yelled Mom. "Just call Sue and Jerry if you need anything!"

"Don't worry about us!" shouted P.J. "Have a good time!" He added under his breath, "Because a good time is just what we're going to have." A moment later, when the car disappeared down the bluff road, he turned toward me with a grin.

"I don't know, P.J.," I said, backing away. "I don't know if this is a good idea."

"Look, you said you wanted to go to one of these big parties, didn't you?"

"Well—"

"This is your chance. What could be easier than having one right at your own house?"

"A root canal, maybe," I muttered, but P.J. was already trotting back toward the house.

It didn't take long for word to spread all over school. Strangers began coming up to me in the hall and saying, "I hear you're having a party." Lots of people asked me for directions. Rachel told me that somebody stood up after the Beta Club's fashion show and said, "Party at P.J.'s. Saturday night." I began to see how it was that hundreds of people showed up at these bashes.

I couldn't believe all these people were coming to our party. What was I going to do if these perfect strangers started walking off with our television or VCR?

P.J. was deeply involved in the mechanics of buying a couple of kegs of beer. "Marty Huber's brother is at State, and Marty says he can get us some kegs," he reported, "but we have to get a truck and go to Raleigh to get them."

"A truck? Just exactly how much beer are we talking about here?"

"It's just that these things are big, Andie. They're, like, barrels." He frowned. "I don't see why we couldn't get them here in town and just give them Dad's charge card number. We can act like they're for a party of Dad's and have the kegs delivered right to the house. That would save a lot of hassle."

"Until Richard got his charge card bill," I pointed out.

"You're right," he said. "I know you're right. I wonder who I could borrow a truck from." He picked up the phone. "You know it's good that Dad and Ellen are going to be gone until Wednesday, because that gives us plenty of time to get the place cleaned up afterward."

"What do you expect to happen to the place that it's going to need cleaning up?" I asked nervously.

"Oh, you know. Cigarette stubs, bottles. Let's face it. People are pigs."

I remembered my precious stuffed animal collection. "I'm going to lock the door to my room," I said.

"Don't worry about it. It'll be mostly on the lawn. People will only go in the house to use the john. I've been to lots of these things."

P.J. obviously didn't understand my point of view, so I went next door to seek moral support from Rachel. I sat down heavily on her bed. "I don't know, Rachel, the whole idea of having three hundred people in the yard just makes me nervous."

"Don't *worry*, Andie! People have these things all the time. It's true that Robbie Hatcher had to pay to have his parents' lawn resodded," she conceded, "but that was only because he started trying to show everybody how to do the Roger Rabbit, and things got out of hand."

I shivered. "But you are going to be there, aren't you, Rache? To give me moral support, I mean."

"Sure. Dooley and I will both be there." She shot a quick glance at her door. "We're leaving early, though. I can't risk being there if things heat up. You know my parents. If I even get *close* to any trouble, I'll be grounded until I graduate."

"Trouble?" I sat up straight. "What kind of trouble?"

"Nothing!" she said hastily. "I didn't mean anything. All I'm saying is that when it comes to booze, my parents are the spiritual descendants of Carry Nation."

"Was she the one who kept taking hatchets to saloons?"

Rachel nodded.

I sighed. "A lady after my own heart."

"I think you're getting the wrong idea, Andie. These parties aren't orgies. Dooley says it's just a bunch of kids standing around talking. Very dull."

"If they're as dull as everybody says, then how come I keep hearing about the police showing up?"

"Naturally with three hundred or so people it can get noisy. I guess the neighbors complain."

"Rachel, your parents *are* the neighbors."

"Don't I know it. That's why I have to watch my step. People drink at these things, you know. And if anybody so much as dumped a beer on me, my life wouldn't be worth living. My parents would never believe I was innocent."

I groaned. "Why does P.J. want to have one of these parties, anyway?"

"Maybe he was brain-damaged at birth?" she suggested.

"No," I said reluctantly. "It's just that he thinks differently from you and me, Rachel. That's what it is. Boys are just different."

She grinned. "I've noticed that."

"I mean they are not rational beings."

"There's no help for it, Andie. P.J.'s going to have this party. You might as well relax and enjoy it."

Easy for her to say.

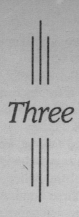

Three

Our backyard was mostly vertical, which is why we had such a great view. But it did let the back out for the party. Our front yard, however, was very large, plenty big enough for the hundreds of people P.J. expected. I was relieved to remember that it was landscaped with pebbles, rocks, pine straw, and a few hardy flowers and bushes. There were no herb gardens and very little grass. So at least P.J. and I would not be faced with having the lawn resodded, an expense which, frankly, I did not see how I could manage on my allowance.

Saturday night we turned on all the outdoor lights, carted out huge bowls of corn chips and jalapeño pepper dip, and put a couple of big coolers of soft drinks next to the kegs.

A few kids showed up around nine. I had never seen them before. Possibly they came from some other town. They stood around awkwardly, talking to one another and sneaking furtive glances at us. Beads of sweat appeared on P.J.'s forehead. "I hope people show up," he said. "I've never been to a party this early, so I don't know if this is the way it usually is. But look at those guys just standing there. It's awful. Where is everybody? What if nobody comes?"

I began to cheer up at that. Maybe there was hope, after all. Maybe nobody would come.

Chris pulled up out front in his mother's car and got out. A blond with a strong resemblance to Malibu Barbie was with him. Since it was only the beginning of March, the girl obviously owned a sunlamp. Either that or she had recently swabbed herself with mahogany shoe polish.

"Hey, Chris," said P.J. "Why didn't you just pull your car into the garage?"

"And get stuck later when the thundering herds show up? No, thanks. You guys know Beezie Lewis?"

Beezie smiled at us. She had excellent white teeth, which contrasted beautifully with her tan.

It amazed me that in spite of Chris's love 'em and leave 'em reputation, he was never short of pretty girls to go out with. Very possibly this was because girls were not rational creatures. Indeed, it would not have totally surprised me if I turned out to be the only rational creature left on earth.

Rachel and Dooley strolled toward us from Rachel's house. We could see them because Rachel's white sweater and pants caught the light. As they got

19

closer I saw the glitter of gold bangles at each of her wrists. She thrust her hands in her pockets and shivered a little. There was a slight chill in the air. "Since we have to leave early, we thought we'd better come over early," she explained.

P.J. glanced at his watch. "Isn't anybody going to show up but my *friends,* for pete's sake."

Just then three carloads of people arrived. It was like those cars of clowns at the circus. Kids kept coming out. I stared. It was unbelievable.

"Aw-right!" said P.J., brightening.

Minutes later the driveway was stacked with cars two abreast and more kept pulling up into the yard. I went to get myself a cola, and by the time I had flipped open the tab, cars were parked halfway down the block.

I looked around the yard. People were standing all over the place in small groups, talking. It was just the way everyone had said. It was dull.

Rachel came up to me holding what looked and smelled like a mug of hot apple cider. "Where did you get that?" I asked enviously.

"At home. Want me to go get you one?"

"No, I'm okay." I glanced around the yard. "When do those things start happening that make the neighbors call the police?"

"What did you expect, Andie? Fireworks?"

I had to admit that I did feel slightly let down that the party was so quiet. I had heard rumors about other parties where girls danced on tables and people got thrown into swimming pools. Of course, we had not put any tables out. Nor did we have a swimming pool. But I had at least expected the scene to be somewhat more animated.

"Of course, I'm relieved that everybody is so well behaved," I said.

"You don't sound relieved," said Rachel.

"Okay, I have mixed feelings, all right? I am curious about life on the wild side. I admit it."

Rachel craned her neck, glancing around. "I wonder if Pete is going to show up."

"Why would Pete show up?" I asked sharply. "This is the last place on earth he'd come."

"Haven't you noticed his car driving past your house a lot lately?"

I had to admit that I had noticed Pete's car a time or two in the past few weeks, which was pretty odd since our neighborhood wasn't on the way to any place else. A single road went up the bluff, wound round the neighborhood houses, and then ended in a cul-de-sac. So what was Pete doing on our street? Where could he be going? It made me nervous to think he was out there hoping to catch a glimpse of me. I had taken to keeping my bedroom blinds closed, but kept telling myself that there had to be some perfectly logical explanation. Maybe he was borrowing class notes from someone in the neighborhood. That was probably it. Just the same, I'd decided to keep my blinds closed.

I sighed. "Why does breaking up have to be so absolutely awful?"

Chris scrambled up on a rock near me. "A very

good question," he said. "I ask myself that all the time."

Abruptly Rachel turned and left. It was possible she felt unable to impartially discuss the subject of breaking up in Chris's presence. She had obviously not forgotten how he had once dumped her.

"So, what's the answer, O World's Greatest Authority on Breaking Up?" I looked up at him.

"Don't get involved in the first place. That's the answer."

"That's what I think too. So, how does that Barbie doll you showed up with tonight fit in?"

Chris leaned toward me and said in a confidential tone, "She doesn't fit in. This is just a casual night out together. It doesn't mean a thing."

"Easy to say," I said sadly. "But what if you picture casual and the other person pictures something else?" That had been my problem with Pete.

"You lay out the ground rules in the beginning. That's the secret. I know I used to say I was good at breaking up, but, heck, all kind of girls aren't speaking to me these days. Did you see the way Rachel cut out of here as soon as I came up?"

I saw what he was getting at. Chris could very possibly have to move to the next state because he had already dated all the girls in this one.

"What I see now," Chris said, "is that I have to make it clear right from the start that this evening means nothing. Zip."

"How? Just how do you do that?" It didn't sound

possible to me, but I was always ready to listen. After all, nobody could claim Chris was inexperienced when it came to the boy-girl scene.

"It's easy. First, never say anything about the future. The future doesn't exist. Second, never get affectionate. 'Nice dress' is as far as it goes with me these days. Third, never say, 'I'll call you.' Fourth, never call." He folded his arms over his chest and looked smug. "I feel pretty positive about this. So far, so good."

"Chris, are you telling me you never make out with these girls?"

"Sure, I make out with them."

"I don't see how you get anybody to go out with you," I said. "I really don't."

"I don't know"—he shrugged—"but so far, no problem."

"Chris?" sang the Barbie doll sweetly.

"Beezie! Hey, do you know Andie?"

If looks could kill I'd have been dead meat. "No," Beezie said coolly. "We haven't met."

Chris reached out and ruffled my hair. "Andie and I are old buddies. I tell her all my troubles."

"He's putting you on," I said. "Chris doesn't have any troubles."

The look in Beezie's eye told me he was fast developing one.

"Chris, would you mind getting me something to drink?" Beezie asked.

Chris slid down from the rock. "Sure. What do you want?"

"Anything as long as it has no sugar, no caffeine, and no alcohol."

This girl didn't take chances. I could admire that. Not only was she into clean living, but she was obviously eager to pry Chris away from my side. I don't think it had dawned on her that this meant she would be stuck talking to me until he returned with her drink. She checked the surface of the rock, brushed it off with her hand, and then sat down on it. The sudden pained expression on her face told me that it had just hit her that she was going to be stuck with me for a while.

"Nice weather we're having," I said.

She ignored my small talk and came right to the point. "I just despise girls who go after other girls' guys, don't you?"

I got her drift all right.

"I didn't know you had anything going with Chris," I said. "I thought this was just a casual date. I figured it meant zip."

Her mouth grew pinched at the corners. "Where'd you get an idea like that?"

"From Chris." I told myself I was only trying to help Chris's project along. That I happened to dislike this girl was purely incidental.

"Of course, Chris and I are just getting to know each other," she admitted. "But we do have an awful lot in common."

Chris appeared at her side with a canned drink.

"Chris!" she cried. "This has got caffeine and sugar both."

"No alcohol, though," he said proudly.

"You drink it." She slid down from the rock. "I'm going to look for something else."

"I didn't see anything with no caffeine."

"How about water?" she snapped.

I tapped him on the shoulder as he turned to follow her. "Don't look now," I whispered, "but I think you've still got a few bugs in your system."

He stuck out his tongue.

Over by the garage a bunch of boys were singing "Waltzing Matilda." I stood for a few minutes listening to them. Then I went indoors and sat down in the family room with a book. I had to admit that so far my experience with life in the fast lane was a disappointment.

I began reading *Pride and Prejudice,* which is one of my all-time favorite books. I was vaguely conscious of people coming and going. The refrigerator door opened a few times. I heard water running and doors opening and closing. But no one stayed inside the house long. Evidently, P.J. was right about people keeping to the outside. Also, nobody tried to carry off the television or VCR. I was sure about that because I sat where I had a clear view of both.

A boy with messy hair stumbled past me. "Which way is the ice?" he muttered.

"In the kitchen. Over there."

The phone rang and I jumped. I hoped it wasn't the neighbors complaining about the noise.

"Want me to get it?" said the guy.

"No!" I yelped. I ran to the phone in the kitchen and grabbed the receiver.

"Andie?" There was crackling on the line.

"Oh, hi, Mom." I gulped.

"How are you and P.J. getting along?"

"Just fine. Absolutely great."

The boy dumped some ice cubes out of the freezer into a bowl. It sounded like twelve bowling balls hitting the deck.

"What was that?" Mom sounded alarmed.

"Nothing. I was just getting some ice cubes out. It's been awfully warm here. I mean, for March." I madly gestured for silence. The boy seemed to catch on because he began elaborately tiptoeing out of the kitchen, holding the bowl of ice cubes.

"We've had beautiful weather, too," said Mom. "Is P.J. there?"

"No, he's, uh, out."

"You're okay there by yourself, aren't you, Andie?" she said fretfully. "I wish P.J. hadn't gone out and left you there alone."

A couple of guys had come in the front door and I heard someone directing them to the kitchen. As soon as they rounded the corner, I propped the phone against my shoulder with my chin and began waving my arms, shooing them away from the kitchen.

"Ice!" one of them said in a stage whisper.

I covered the receiver with my hand. "Go away!" I hissed. "This is my mother on the phone."

"Andie?" Mom's voice came from the receiver. "Are you there?"

"I'm here, Mom. This is kind of a bad connection."

"You sound out of breath. Are you okay?"

"I just had to run for the phone. I was in the family room reading."

One of the guys began tiptoeing past me. Suddenly his legs slid out from under him and he landed flat on his bottom. An ice cube skidded from under his feet and flew across the floor.

"Andie?" cried Mom in alarm. "What was that noise?"

"The television," I said. "I guess I have it on too loud."

"I thought you were reading."

"I was. But it's so spooky here when it's quiet. That's why I turned on the set." I was pretty proud of the way I kept coming up with answers.

The guy on the floor rubbed his head and swore.

"You poor thing," said Mom. "I knew we shouldn't have left you there alone."

"No, no, Mom. I'm fine. Really. P.J. will be coming in any minute. I think he just went to a friend's house to study or something. We're getting along great."

I eyed the guy on the floor nervously. He was holding on to a kitchen chair and trying to pull himself up. I just hoped he didn't snare the cord of the toaster with his foot.

"Well, we'll be home in a couple of days, anyway," said Mom.

"Great. Don't let me run up your phone bill."

"You're right. I'm afraid this is costing a fortune."

The toaster crashed to the floor. The guy on the floor looked totally surprised. You would have thought he was some aborigine who had never seen an electric cord.

"I'd better go, Mom."

"I think you'd better turn down that television, Andie. We don't want the neighbors to get upset."

"Right, Mom. I'll do that. Right away."

"I love you, sweetheart. Tell P.J. we were sorry to have missed him."

"I'll tell him."

I hung up and glared at the guys slinking out of the kitchen. "That was my mother on the phone, you jerks," I said. "I could murder you!"

"Couldn't we just get a little ice first?" one of them asked.

"Honestly!" I went back to the family room and opened my book. I was not exactly calm; my pulse was setting new records. But I thought that on the whole I had handled the situation pretty well.

P.J. stuck his head into the family room. "I think one of us ought to go out and get more ice," he said. "The cooler's just about empty."

"Not me. I've done my part. That was Mom on the phone."

"Jeez." He paled. "How'd it go?"

"Okay, but it didn't help any that guys were tearing through the kitchen sounding like colliding garbage trucks."

"Did she suspect anything?"

"I told her it was the television."

"Good thinking." He brightened. "I knew my luck was still holding."

I thought I deserved a little of the credit, but I was in no mood to argue.

"I guess I'll go get a bag of ice," he said.

"Fine. Do that." I turned the page of my book. After a while I was once more lost in the elegant world of Jane Austen. I'm not sure at what point I became aware that the noise level from outside was heightened. But after a while I began to notice an awful lot of racket. I closed my book and crept to the front door. Cautiously I cracked the door and peeked out. Some boys were trying to form a human pyramid beside the driveway, or maybe they were trying to fight but were too drunk to do more than crawl over one another. Most of the other kids were gathered around them in a circle. I wasn't sure if they were placing bets or what. A car parked out front had all its doors open and its sound system was going full blast. I looked around for Rachel and Dooley, but then remembered they planned to leave early. Chris's car was gone too. I checked my watch and was shocked that it was almost midnight already.

A guy wearing a painter's hat turned backward began clambering up the rock where Chris had been sitting earlier. When he stood up, I saw he had something glittering in his hand. A blast rent the air, and a moment later I realized the guy was playing taps on a trumpet. It didn't go with the rock music blaring from the open car, but for anybody who likes discordant sound effects, it must have been a real treat.

Near me, on the front stoop, a guy in shredded jeans was kissing a girl wearing a T-shirt with Camp Winnahaukee on the front. Her jacket slipped off her shoulders and she giggled.

P.J. inched through the door past me. "We need more soft drinks. Are all the Doritos gone?"

"Of course the Doritos are gone, P.J.," I said patiently. "It's almost midnight. How long did you expect them to last? To the year 2000?"

"Have you been reading a *book?*" P.J. stared. He acted as if he'd never seen one before.

"I was, but I think I may have to go upstairs and put a pillow over my head instead." I put down my book on the hall table and covered my ears.

"It's going pretty well, don't you think?"

That was when I spotted the blinking blue lights. I plucked at P.J.'s shirtsleeve. "Look!" As the police car paused in front of our house, blue light flickered on car bumpers and colored people's faces. There was a stirring of panic in the yard.

"Jeez," said P.J. "It's the cops."

"What happens now?"

"Nothing much." P.J. looked uncertain. "I guess they'll just tell everybody to go home"—he hesitated—"I think." After a second he added, "I hope."

A tall boy standing near us dropped the can he was holding and crushed it under his foot.

A couple of police officers strode into the yard. One of them climbed up on the rock. I could see the flashing blue light reflected in his shiny black boots. "Party's over!" he shouted. "You've got ten minutes to clear the premises."

"Does that mean we have to leave?" I whispered to P.J.

"Don't be stupid, Andie," snapped P.J. "We live here."

He was right, of course. I don't know what it is, but authority figures with black boots and guns rattle me.

I sensed a lot of movement outside and heard the rumble of engines as kids started their cars.

"I hope nobody's stupid enough to drive drunk." P.J. nudged me. "Look down the road. There's the other cop car waiting to pick up kids."

"You don't think they're going to do anything to us, do you?" I was aware that my voice was squeaking, but I couldn't help it. Terror has that effect on me.

"What can they do to us?" P.J. shrugged uneasily. "We're sober. We're on our own property. Can we help it if a bunch of jerks come party on our front lawn?"

"Of course not," I said, trying to sound confident. "We can't help it one little bit."

A boy in a windbreaker squeezed past us. "Excuse me," he said politely.

I heard doors opening and closing behind me in the house.

P.J. looked around vaguely. Neither of us was sure what etiquette dictates when one's party is raided.

A police officer moved toward us, kicking a can out

of his way. "You're going to have quite a mess to clean up, son," he said. "I hope this is going to be a lesson to you."

"Yes, sir." P.J. gulped. "I guess I didn't expect so many people to show up."

The cop glared at us a second. I thought I heard him mutter, "Crazy kids." Then he stomped away.

We stood there for a while watching people clear out. P.J.'s face was pasty white, and I expect I didn't look too great myself.

"Jeez." P.J. blinked rapidly. "The ten minutes are up and there are still cars out there. You think people are passed out in the bushes?"

It was certainly possible.

"And look at all that junk in the yard. Can you believe it?"

There did seem to be a lot of paper cups and cans lying around. The outside lights didn't give off a lot of candlepower, but I could make out mounds of debris.

Glancing at P.J., I sensed this was not the moment to say "I told you so."

I retrieved my book. "I don't know about you," I said, "but I'm tired."

I left P.J. in the foyer and went into the kitchen to fix myself some hot chocolate in the microwave. Maybe it was nerves, but my hands were cold. Face it, I thought. You are not cut out for life in the fast lane. Thinking about it for a moment, I decided I could live with that personal limitation.

I gulped down my cocoa, then went upstairs, picking up a can on the way. Something told me that in broad daylight the place was going to look even worse, but I decided to worry about that later.

Once I got to my room I dropped the can in the wastebasket, undressed, put on my bathrobe, and went into my bathroom. When I pulled the shower curtains back, I screamed. A boy was standing in my bathtub. I backed out of the bathroom, clutching my bathrobe together.

P.J. came thundering upstairs. "What's wrong, Andie?"

I sat down abruptly on my bed, my heart pounding like a bass drum. "Th-there's a boy in my bathtub," I managed to say finally.

P.J. blanched. "Is he dead?"

The boy appeared at the door of the bathroom. "Hey, man!" he said. "I'm sorry about that. I didn't mean to scare you or anything."

"Jordan," P.J. yelped. "Get the heck out of here. What do you think you're doing in my sister's bathroom?"

Jordan hiccupped, then raised his hand to cover his mouth. "I didn't think I'd better drive," he said sheepishly. "That's how they got old Brian, you know."

"Well, you can't stay here, man. Move it! Get out of here."

"Are the cops gone yet?"

P.J. hesitated. "I don't know. Wait downstairs a minute. I guess I can drive you home."

"Thanks," Jordan said warmly. "I appreciate that, man."

We heard his uncertain steps going downstairs.

I bent over and looked under the bed. To my relief, no one was hiding under it. "Check my closet, P.J., would you?"

He didn't laugh. He checked the closet. "All clear. You better get some clothes on, Andie. We're going to have to search the house. And I mean the whole house. Jordan probably isn't the only one who got the idea of hiding out until the cops left."

"Do you mean these people are going to be popping out at us from all over the place from now on?"

"We're going to *find* them. That's why we search, right?"

I took a deep breath. "Right."

We found one guy throwing up in P.J.'s bathroom. A girl with long brown hair was shivering in the broom closet near the kitchen. "Have you seen Bill Talbot?" she asked me.

"Try the downstairs powder room," I said. "We've already been through the upstairs."

The house was large and on three levels, so it took us some time to search it. The final total from our dragnet was five boys and two girls, most of them scared into being almost sober.

"Can't you drive me home yet, P.J.?" Jordan asked plaintively. "I don't want to be here all night."

"Shut up," growled P.J. "Anybody else need a ride?"

"Me," piped up the broom closet girl. "I need a ride. It looks like Bill drove off without me."

"Jeez," said P.J. in disgust. "Why are people such pigs?"

I stifled a yawn. "Do you think I can go up and go to bed now?"

"I guess so," said P.J. "I *think* that we've found them all."

I blinked. "Uh, on second thought, I think I'll go with you."

The girl's name was Pamela. She didn't say much as we drove her to Morningside Heights subdivision. Nobody said much. We turned in at the colonial-style brick pillars that marked the subdivision entrance, and P.J. drove up to Pamela's carport to let her out. Jordan lived miles from Pamela and in the exact opposite direction, natch. To get to his place we had to drive through the deserted center of town. Office buildings glowed faintly where lights had been left on to discourage burglaries. A frightened cat streaked across our path. Finally, a half mile past town, we got to Greenwood subdivision. Our head-lights shone on a planting of daffodils as we dropped Jordan off in front of his house. "And don't forget to come get your car tomorrow," P.J. warned him.

"No problem," Jordan said. "Hey, you guys are the greatest, you know?"

P.J. slammed the car door closed and we drove away. "What time is it?" he asked me.

I shook my watch. Judging from the way my head hurt, I half expected dawn to break momentarily. "After one."

35

P.J. sighed. "We can't sleep too late tomorrow, you know. We've got a lot of cleaning up to do."

We? I thought. *We* have cleaning up to do? I didn't say anything though. It was very important for me to stay on P.J.'s good side. I just had to keep reminding myself of that.

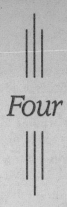

Four

Dooley, Chris, and Rachel all showed up on Sunday to help us clean. It was a good thing. Even with everybody working, it took us the entire day. When we finished we had two big leaf bags full of aluminum cans out by the curb.

After school the next day P.J. went by Green Meadows Nursery and bought a small pine tree to replace the one somebody had backed a car over. He also picked up a few azaleas. Some of ours had unaccountably gotten trampled. After we got the new plants put in, he raked the pebbles out front into neat swirls. But even at that he wasn't happy. He went inside and remade all the beds to give the sheets hospital corners. Next I caught him burning incense in his bathroom. "I know we scrubbed it, but it still smells funny in here," he insisted.

"'All the perfumes of Araby will not sweeten this little hand,'" I intoned.

"What?"

"It's a line from *Macbeth*," I explained. "After the Macbeths commit murder, Lady Macbeth keeps getting the feeling she has blood on her hands, but no matter how much she washes them they still feel the same. It's because of her guilty conscience."

"I don't have blood on my hands, Andie," he snapped.

"I know, I know. I didn't mean anything by it. It's just a quotation."

"Look, I actually drove stupid Jordan home and that dumb girl too. Didn't I? And I've just about killed myself cleaning the house. Are you trying to say I should feel guilty or something?"

"No! Nothing like that. Honest."

"Well, all right, then."

But you do feel guilty, I thought. Or something.

The funny thing about it was that normally P.J. was the farthest thing from a neatness nut. I had seen him, when finishing a package of corn chips, actually stuff the cellophane wrapper between the sofa cushions. He left dirty socks all over the house, even in the kitchen, and his room could have been declared a disaster area. Personally, I was amazed to learn that he knew how to make a bed at all, much less with hospital corners.

"You don't think the Greens are going to tell Dad and Ellen about the party, do you?" His brow puckered anxiously. "Rachel didn't seem to know."

"I don't think Rachel's mother is the type to interfere," I said. As far as I could tell, Mrs. Green was a quiet woman who was devoted to her collection of Oriental porcelain. "I don't think she'll come running over here with the news. On the other hand, if they *ask* her—"

"Why would they ask? The house is perfect. The yard is perfect. Nobody got arrested. This was a perfect cr—I mean, party."

"You're right," I said. "You have absolutely nothing to worry about."

"*We* have absolutely nothing to worry about," he corrected me.

There it was, that "we" of his. It seemed to evaporate when it came to discussing the use of the car, but it magically reappeared whenever there was unpleasantness to share. P.J. could be very annoying.

Mom and Richard's car drove into the garage Wednesday afternoon. When we heard them, we threw open the kitchen door and pasted matching bright smiles on our faces.

"Did you have fun?" I called down to them.

"I bet I put on ten pounds," moaned Richard. He hoisted the suitcases out of the trunk. Even in the dim light of the garage, I could see that he had a sunburn.

"It's funny," said Mom as she mounted the steps. "We've only been gone a week, but somehow everything looks different. Like the yard . . ." Her voice trailed off.

"Here, let me help you with those bags, Dad," said P.J. hastily. He ran past Mom and wrested the suitcases out of Richard's hands.

"Hey, I'm not *that* tired," protested Richard. "Your old dad's not completely feeble yet, you know."

"Just trying to help," said P.J.

Mom stepped into the kitchen and sniffed. "What's that smell?"

"Oh, that? Uh, pine disinfectant, I guess."

"You scrubbed the floor?" She looked at me, surprised.

"We spilled some milk," I said glibly.

P.J. staggered in with the suitcases.

"It sure is great to be home," said Richard.

Mom and Richard glanced around the family room, slightly puzzled. You would have thought they had taken inventory and found something missing. But nothing was missing. We had been over the place with the most extreme care. Absolutely nothing was out of order. "Well," Mom said finally. "The place certainly is neat."

"We're just glad you had a good trip." P.J. was anxious to change the subject. "Did you get seasick?"

"No," said Mom, glancing around absently. "We didn't get seasick. It was all very nice."

"Great," said P.J. "Well, I guess I'd better go over to Chris's now."

"What do you mean you're going over to Chris's?" said Richard. "We just got home."

"I have to borrow his chemistry notes," explained P.J.

I didn't believe P.J.'s story about the chemistry notes for a minute. For one thing, I had never known him to study chemistry. It was obvious to me that his nerve was buckling and he had to escape. I had seen his eyes checking over the room anxiously, looking for any telltale can or bottle that we might have overlooked. The strain was beginning to take its toll on him. "See you," he said. He exited hastily.

Richard went upstairs to unpack, but Mom sat down and fixed me with an intent gaze. "Andie, honey, is there anything you need to tell me?"

"No. Nothing." My heart jumped up into my throat and throbbed there. "Why do you ask?"

"I don't know. I just have a funny feeling. P.J. seemed kind of strange just now, didn't you think?"

"P.J. *is* strange, Mom."

"Oh, nonsense." She stifled a yawn and leaned her head on her hand. "Maybe I'm just tired. I guess I'd better just go upstairs and unpack."

"That sounds like a good idea." I cleared my throat. "Mom, I think I'll go over to Rachel's—if that's okay. She and I need to study French."

I ran up to my room and got my books. When I stepped out into the hall, I could hear Mom and Richard talking in their room. Unfortunately, the door was closed and I couldn't tell what they were saying. But why was I worried? There wasn't anything they possibly *could* say. The house was in apple-pie shape.

Unable to quell my jumpy feeling, I went over to Rachel's. Maybe it was my imagination, but it seemed to me that Mrs. Green studied me closely when I went in. I had the uneasy feeling she thought I was one of those who had been acting wild the night of the party. I wanted to explain that I had spent most of the evening reading *Pride and Prejudice,* but I didn't have a chance to speak. The phone rang at the back of the house, and she hurried off to get it. I went on up to Rachel's room. "I am not cut out for a life of crime," I said, shutting the door behind me.

"What crime? What's going on, Andie?" Rachel was on the bed, a book propped against her knees.

I cleared away the papers at the foot of her bed and sat down. "Mom and Richard just got home, and they're acting awfully suspicious."

"It's just your guilty conscience."

"Get this. Mom said to me, 'Andie, honey, is there anything you need to tell me?' Is that unnerving or what?"

"Well, good grief, Andie, if you go around shaking like a leaf and looking behind you, naturally she's going to wonder what's going on."

"I'm no good at this. I freely admit it. Rache, was it your parents who called the police?"

"I think it was the Harpers down the street. Also the Masons. At least, that's what Mrs. Mason told Mom."

"I may kill myself."

"What's the big deal? You were just an innocent bystander. You haven't done anything wrong."

"There is such a thing as guilt by association, you know. I notice you were pretty paranoid about hanging around the party yourself."

"My parents can be very unreasonable," Rachel said primly. "Look, everything's going to be fine. Why would they suspect anything? Calm down, will you? We've got to study this French."

"You're right." I took a deep breath. "We've got to study this French."

I actually succeeded in concentrating so hard on irregular verbs that I almost forgot to worry about what was going on at home. I suppose I recognized that Rachel was right and that part of the problem was my oversensitive conscience. Obviously, I was going to have to learn to deal with that better if I intended to keep trailing along with P.J. and his friends.

When I got home, I heard shouting coming from the kitchen. I stuck my head in. "Hello?" I said.

Richard was pacing the floor, as is his habit when he is stirred up. P.J. was sitting under the kitchen light looking like a victim of police interrogation.

"Andie," Mom said grimly, "we've been talking to the Greens just now."

So that was why the Greens' phone had been ringing when I stepped into Rachel's house. I froze.

"P.J. tells us you didn't have anything to do with what happened," said Richard.

"Though," said Mom, "it seems to me you obviously must have aided and abetted—"

Richard held up his hand. "I can understand how you didn't want to squeal on P.J., Andie, and I don't expect it."

"I don't know about that," muttered Mom.

"Suffice it to say," said Richard, "we are disappointed."

"Very disappointed," echoed Mom.

I thought guiltily about how I had lied when Mom called home. It was true that I had aided and abetted. She was right.

"It's just lucky no one was hurt," Richard said. "This could have been very serious."

"I knew it was a mistake to leave them here alone," said Mom. "I told you so."

"There's no point in going into that now, El," snapped Richard. "The important thing is that P.J. has to realize that his actions have consequences."

P.J. didn't say anything, but he looked as if he were going down for the third time. I didn't feel so great myself.

"Why don't you go up to your room, Andie?" suggested Richard. "P.J. and I are not finished talking."

"I don't see why Andie should get off without being punished," protested Mom.

I felt myself go cold. What kind of punishment did she have in mind? Were they going to yank the car? Was I going to have to ride the bus to school from now on?

"We can talk about that later," said Richard. "Upstairs, Andie."

I went up to my room right away and called Rachel.

"Why are you whispering?" she said when she picked up the phone. "Speak up!"

"Your parents spilled the beans," I said. "P.J.'s

downstairs being beaten with rubber hoses right now."

"Ye gods. What are they going to do to you?"

"They have another plan for me. They're going to kill me with suspense."

"Oh, come on, Andie."

"Richard thinks I'm innocent, which I am, sort of. I mean, it's not like the party was my idea. I just went along with it so as to stay on P.J.'s good side. But Mom doesn't want Richard thinking she's too easy on me, so she keeps saying I ought to be punished."

"This could get nasty."

"It already *is* nasty."

"Well, just hang in there. This is probably the worst part. They haven't had time to cool down yet."

I hoped she was right.

A while later I heard P.J. coming upstairs alone. I ran to my door and peeked out. "What happened?" I asked anxiously.

He came into my room. His cowlick was standing straight up and the skin of his face looked tightly stretched over his skull. "I'm grounded for the fore-seeable future. And if I get into any more trouble, I have to go live with my mother." He made a face.

P.J.'s mom had married an army colonel, who was currently stationed in Germany. P.J. hated his step-father, who thought it was a sad day when the armed services gave up flogging. If P.J. had to go live with his mom and the colonel, not only would he have to put up with the monster, he would have to leave all his friends. Also, he would not have a car, and he would have to go to school right on the army base, a fate he considered worse than death.

"That's bad," I said sympathetically.

He shrugged. "It's not going to happen. It's not as if I can get into any more trouble now even if I wanted to. What kind of trouble can I get into when I'm grounded?"

"But you'll hate being grounded."

He managed a weak smile. "So, it could be good for me. I'll have lots of time on my hands. Maybe my grades will even come up."

"Look, P.J., I really appreciate your sticking up for me the way you did. Saying it wasn't my fault and all."

"Yeah, but it was the truth, Andie. It wasn't really your party. Besides, what good would it do me if they grounded you too?"

I was still grateful. Suppose he had taken the line that it had been my idea, that I had led him astray? I shivered at the thought.

"You win some, you lose some," said P.J.

I shot him an admiring look. To be grounded for the indefinite future and still be able to be philosophical about it, that was true cool. "The only thing I can't figure out," I said, "is how they guessed."

"Oh, they told me that," he said bitterly. "It was because everything looked so clean. Ellen said that as soon as she walked in the house and saw how neat it was, she knew something had happened."

I winced. "Oh, no! We overdid it!"

"Looks like it." He shrugged. "I'm not allowed to get any phone calls or make any phone calls or have any visitors, and I can't go anywhere except school. It's going to be interesting, kind of like being exiled to Siberia." He produced a sickly smile.

"You've never been grounded before?"

"Well, sure. For a day or two. Once for a whole week. But nothing like this."

"Maybe they'll cool down later."

"Maybe." When I thought about the Gothic scene downstairs, I could sort of understand why P.J. didn't expect any mercy. And for somebody who could quite legitimately be called a party animal, I thought he was taking it amazingly well. In fact, he was taking it so well it was almost spooky.

A little later, though, after he had gone to his room, I heard muffled thuds coming from that direction. It sounded very much as if he was kicking the wall.

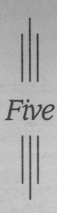

Five

Around five o'clock I drove to the mall. I was aching to get out, and nobody stopped me from leaving the house. Instead of a formal punishment Mom and Richard had simply decided to be very stiff and cold with me. I had the feeling I would be spending a lot of time at the mall in the near future. Compared to the way things were at home, it seemed to be pulsing with human warmth.

I sat down in the snack plaza and surveyed the menu on the wall. I wasn't feeling enthusiastic about food, but after a while I got up and got a slice of pizza just to have some excuse for sitting at a table. When I got back and sat down, everything went black.

"Chris!" I said. "Stop it."

He took his hands off my eyes. "How did you know it was me, Andie?"

"Because it always is. That's how."

He pulled up a chair. "What's the matter? You look terrible."

"Mom and Richard are home and they know everything." I filled him in on the gruesome details.

"P.J. grounded!" he keened. "I can't believe it!"

"Believe it. It's true." I thought about P.J.'s closed bedroom door. That was one of the reasons I had to get out of the house. That closed door gave me morbid fantasies, like maybe P.J. was in there slashing his wrists or something.

"Jeez, he might as well be dead," said Chris, uncannily echoing my thoughts.

"I can carry messages to him for you. He's still allowed to speak to me. At least, as far as I can make out."

"This is terrible. Worse than terrible. It's a disaster."

We sat in gloom for a couple of minutes before Chris spoke again.

"You know something, Andie, I think Rachel is turning Dooley against me."

"Oh, no, Chris. I'm sure you're wrong about that."

"Yeah, but Dooley's never around anymore."

"He's always off with Rachel, that's all."

"Amounts to the same thing. And now P.J. is out of commission too." He sighed. "This is serious. Who am I going to hang out with?"

"I'm sure you'll be able to find some girl or another to keep you company."

"Very funny. Ha-ha."

"I wasn't kidding."

He lifted a bit of pepperoni off my pizza and met my eyes. "Think about it. As fast as they come and go lately, I barely get a chance to catch their names."

"Ah, yes, your new plan for pain-free romance— the superquick turnover. How's it working out?"

"Not so good. I've got some problems with it. You know, I *like* girls. I like to have them around."

"Nah! You're putting me on!"

"Cut it out, Andie. You aren't helping any."

"Sorry." I lowered my gaze and stirred my drink with my straw.

"It's just that I don't like flagging down someone new every time I want a date," he complained. "It's wearing me out, and it's not much fun."

"It beats going with someone," I said fervently. "Nothing could induce me to get into that again. Never. It's not worth the pain."

"You're right. I know that. Like right now, you and me can sit here together and split this slice of pizza with no problem. But if either of us was going with somebody it would mean a bad scene. Next thing you know they'd be on the phone saying, 'So and so saw you with such and such.' And then it'd be 'Waaaah, I hate your guts.'"

"I was thinking exactly the same thing."

Chris scowled. "So why aren't we happy?"

I sighed. "It's this stuff with P.J. I really feel awful about what happened. I should have tried to talk him out of that party."

"Nobody could have talked him out of that party, Andie."

As a matter of fact, Chris and Dooley had actually egged him on. But there was no point in bringing that up now.

"I know," I said, "but I still feel awful."

"Look, are you going to eat that pizza?"

I stared down at it distastefully. I always lose my appetite when things go wrong. Life being what it is, that keeps me more or less permanently underweight. "I guess not," I said.

"I'll take it off your hands then," said Chris. He tore a large bite out of it, and a glob of mozzarella dripped onto the table. "Things will look better tomorrow," he promised me.

One thing you could count on about Chris—he was an incurable optimist. I envied that.

When P.J. and I got home from school the next Monday, Mom was in the kitchen waiting to make sure P.J. came in on time. Richard was the one with all the rigid ideas about what constituted being truly grounded, but Mom was stuck with being chief jailer. She didn't like it, but it was clear that she was determined to be conscientious about it. I saw her glance at the clock as we walked in the door.

"Kids, this is Lupe," said Mom. I was startled to see that a girl with long black hair was standing at the kitchen sink scraping carrots. "She's going to be helping out around the house," Mom said. "She'll live in the attic room until she saves up for a car and finds an apartment."

Our house had a sort of room for servants with its own outside entrance. But as far as I knew it hadn't been used in years, and it was always locked. If Lupe was going to stay there, Mom must have been in a flurry that day pounding rugs and fluffing pillows to make it livable.

Lupe turned to take us in with large frightened eyes. "Hi," she said.

"Hi," I said. There was something exotic about the rich coil of black hair that prompted me to ask, "Are you from around here?"

She smiled at me nervously and licked her lips.

"Lupe doesn't understand much English," Mom said. "Why don't you kids take your books upstairs. We're going to try to keep things neater around here from now on, and Lupe doesn't need the extra work of picking up after us."

P.J. shot me a look. I knew how he felt. Who could have guessed that when we cleaned up the house so carefully we were spurring Mom on to these extreme measures? Up to now we had lived in a household where corn chip packages, socks, and panty hose could be strewn about without anyone getting wrought up about them. Suddenly that was changing, and P.J. and I were too thoroughly demoralized to protest.

Mom followed us upstairs. I suppose she was watching in case P.J. tried to slip out the front door.

"Why do we have to have a maid all of a sudden?" I asked.

"The house looked so nice after you kids cleaned it up"—Mom paused and frowned—"I guess what's more to the point was that it looked radically *different*. Richard and I realized then that the cleaning service wasn't doing a good enough job. I suppose to be fair about it, two mornings a week isn't enough in a house this big, so we decided we should try to get someone full-time. We were really lucky to get Lupe. Everyone tells me that help is hard to find, so when I went to the employment agency and saw Lupe in the waiting room, I snapped her up. Luckily, they had an interpreter on hand. The only drawback is that she doesn't speak much English, but I think we can manage. I stopped off and bought a Spanish-English dictionary."

Mom seemed to have forgotten that P.J. knew some Spanish. True, he made Ds, but this was his second year, and presumably he had absorbed *something*. P.J. didn't bother to remind her. He was even more uncommunicative than usual these past few days. He ate his breakfast without saying a word. He ate his dinner without saying a word. Just now he had walked upstairs ahead of us without saying a word. As soon as Mom disappeared into her room, however, P.J. turned to me, grinned, and said "Va-voom!"

I blinked. "Would you care to translate?"

"Those eyes!" he said enthusiastically. "Those legs!"

"Mom's?" I asked blankly.

"No, stupid. Lupe's."

"I didn't notice. All I saw was that she looked scared."

"We've got to make her feel at home," said P.J., smirking.

I cast a nervous glance at Mom's door. "P.J., Mom is not going to like it if you start hitting on the hired help. Believe me. She would think you were taking advantage of Lupe. This is a surefire method to get yourself a one-way ticket to Germany."

He widened his eyes. "Who said anything about hitting on Lupe?"

"Excuse me. I somehow got that idea. I apologize."

"Apology accepted. Look here, Andie, nobody can complain if I want to practice my Spanish, can they?" He opened the door to his room and smiled at me over his shoulder. "I need to bring up those grades in Spanish anyway."

Behind the closed door I heard him whistling. Under the circumstances his whistling seemed almost more ominous than the silence that had bothered me before.

I went into my room and called Rachel.

"Mom has hired a maid," I told her.

"I've heard all about it. My mother is so jealous she called my dad at work to complain."

"This girl doesn't speak much English."

"That's good. That way you won't feel like she's eavesdropping. Personally, I wouldn't want a full-time maid. I mean part-time help is one thing, but it would give me the creeps to have some stranger living in the house."

"Thanks a lot, Rachel. I can always count on you to say something comforting."

"Of course, you're used to living with strangers. It hasn't been that long ago since you moved in with Richard and P.J.—and you hardly knew them at all."

"That was ages ago, and I sure know them now."

"Well, I guess you'll get to know the maid too. If she stays around long enough."

"What makes you think she's going to leave?"

"Ask yourself if you'd want to spend your life picking up P.J.'s smelly socks. As soon as she learns English, she'll be out of there."

"I hope she learns fast."

"You don't like her?"

"I don't even know her." I glanced at my closed door. "But what worries me is that P.J. is more than usually interested in her—if you follow me."

Rachel was nothing if not quick on the uptake. "She must be pretty good-looking."

"She's not bad looking. But the thing that really worries me is that P.J. is stuck in the house night and day. He's not allowed to talk to anybody but Mom and Richard and me. And Mom and Richard are so mad at him they hardly even look at him, so it's practically like solitary confinement. I think he's about ready to crack, and it's only been a few days. He could be capable of just about anything."

"It was really stupid of your mom to hire someone young and good-looking."

"You don't seem to understand how serious this is," I said. "If P.J. steps out of line, they're going to send him off to live with his mother!"

"How about that?" Rachel sounded pleased. "Do you realize that if they did, you'd get to have the car *all* the time."

"I don't want the car all the time. No, wait a minute. Let me rephrase that. I mean, sure, I'd like to have the car more often, but I don't want P.J. to get sent off to Germany just to get it."

"Good grief, Andie. It seems like all you do is complain about him."

"That's not true. Besides, I take it all back. I just realized that I would miss him. It's spooky enough when he holes up in his room. Imagine what it would be like if he were gone for good!"

"Look, I'll bet you're probably blowing this all out of proportion."

"Sure. You're the one who said I was worrying too much about the party, and look what happened. Catch me listening to you."

"Okay, make yourself miserable if that's what makes you happy!" Rachel hung up.

I wasn't sure exactly what I had expected of Rachel, but a little more warm concern would have been nice. Next I called Chris. Fortunately, he took the whole situation much more seriously than Rachel had.

"Is she really that good-looking?" he asked.

"She's not bad. She's—pretty."

"I better come over there and check her out."

"You can't do that, Chris. You know that P.J. isn't allowed to have his friends over."

"Use your brain, Andie. For purposes of this visit I'm *your* friend."

"I don't know—"

"I'll be there in five minutes."

After I hung up I ran to Mom's study and knocked on the door. "Come in!" she yelled. She turned away from the computer and scowled at me. "Can't this wait, Andie? I'm not getting anything done. I already lost all kinds of time getting Lupe set up."

"I just wanted to ask if Chris can come over."

"You know that P.J. can't entertain his friends when he's grounded."

"Yes, but Chris is *my* friend too."

Mom hesitated. I suppose she was wondering what Richard would say about Chris coming over. "I guess it'll be okay," she said finally, "as long as P.J. stays in his room and doesn't come down to join you."

"No problem." I smiled and closed the door.

Next I ran upstairs and told P.J. he couldn't come downstairs as long as Chris was in the house.

"I can't believe this," he said. "You're telling me Chris is going to be right downstairs, and I have to stay up here twiddling my thumbs? I can't even go into my own kitchen? Who thought this up? Is this some special refined kind of torture?" He frowned. "Anyway, if I can't come down, what's Chris coming over here for?"

"He wants to see Lupe."

57

"Tell him hands off," said P.J. sharply. "She's taken."

"Honestly, P.J.!"

"Don't preach to me, Andie, until *you* try being grounded."

"I'm sorry. I'm really truly sorry that you're grounded."

"I can't believe it," he said bitterly. "This is a black comedy or something."

I noticed he wasn't laughing. I quickly backed out of his room.

A few minutes later Chris bounded up the stairs from the garage. "Where is she?" he asked as soon as I opened the kitchen door.

"Shh." I glanced behind me. Lupe, wearing a fuzzy mitt on her hand, was carefully dusting the venetian blinds in the family room. It was probably the first time they had been dusted.

Chris stepped inside and looked her up and down. "A clear and present danger," he murmured.

"Shh." I frowned. I wasn't sure how much English Lupe understood.

Mom came wafting out of her study. "Hullo, Chris."

I stared at her in disbelief. Mom hardly ever came out to chat during working hours. But unbelievably, there she was. I supposed she was checking to make sure P.J. hadn't sneaked downstairs to see Chris.

"Hi, Mrs. G.," said Chris.

"How's school?" she asked.

"Fine." Chris grabbed my hand. "Andie and I are going to go out and get some supper, okay?"

"We are?" I was startled. Chris kicked me. "We are," I said. "We're going out to get a bite to eat."

"That's fine." She smiled. "Have fun." Before Mom returned to the study, she peeked into the foyer and checked the stairs to make sure P.J. wasn't trying to sneak down.

A minute later we were in Chris's car speeding down the bluff. "No wonder P.J.'s freaking out," Chris said. "That's the worst, man. I've never known your mom to come out like that. I always thought she was chained to the computer in there or something. I guess she's watching P.J.'s every move, huh?"

"That's about the size of it. Richard's probably warned her to make sure P.J. doesn't get away with anything."

Chris shuddered. "That's grim. It's like being under house arrest."

"So, what do you think?" I asked. "You really think Lupe is good-looking?"

"How can you ask? Those smoldering eyes, that shy smile, those lips full of promise—"

"Oh, good grief, Chris."

"I'm just trying to convey the flavor of the male response."

"I get the drift. You don't have to convey any more."

"Anyway, I think you're right about what you said. P.J. is in a bad situation. He can't talk to his friends, can't blow off steam. This kind of thing could drive a person to do anything. You'd better keep an eye on him, Andie."

"Mom's already keeping an eye on him. I don't think he needs any more eyes on him."

"You're right. He's a desperate man. We don't want to make things worse." Chris put his arm on the back of the seat and let it fall to my shoulders. I looked at him in surprise.

"I'm just trying to think like a desperate man," he explained.

"I see."

"And it isn't difficult," he said mournfully.

Chris had a hard time keeping his hands off any girl, even me and I was just a friend. I decided to take the arm around me as a friendly gesture. I needed Chris. When it came to problems with P.J., he was the best listener I had.

"What do you think?" My eyes searched his face anxiously. "Maybe we're making too much of what P.J. said. You know, when I think about it, it's not like P.J. was some notorious ladies' man."

He drew away from me. "Is that a slam, Andie?"

"Getting awfully sensitive, aren't you?"

"Nah," he said lightly. "I knew you couldn't be talking about me."

"Look, you do follow what I'm saying, don't you? I mean, if it were you, it would be one thing. But with P.J. it's all talk. He hasn't made a move toward a girl since Suzy broke up with him."

"I hope you're right. But we've got to be alert. If there's going to be trouble, the big thing is that we've got to see it before your mother does."

I let my head rest on the back of the seat. Lights were whizzing by outside, clear and bright in the cool air. I was already feeling a lot better. "I think maybe I overreacted," I said. "It's really doing me good to talk about it."

We pulled up at the Pizza Hut. There are never many kids there on week nights so we didn't have any trouble finding a booth. The only people in the place were families with kids. The jukebox wasn't even playing.

"This can be my treat," Chris announced.

"We can split it. You don't think they'd cut off my allowance, do you?" I considered it briefly. "Nah, they wouldn't do that. I'll pay my half."

"Yeah, but I owe you for that pizza slice of yours I ate at the mall, remember?"

The waitress brought us a small pepperoni and mushroom. I surprised myself by being hungry. The funny thing was that now that Chris was taking my worries about P.J. seriously, I began to see that I was letting my imagination run away with me. Was it really likely that P.J. would flirt with Lupe so flagrantly that Mom and Richard would pack him off to Germany? Put like that, the whole idea seemed absurd.

If I was more optimistic than I had been earlier, I think it was primarily because of Chris. It was not just that he was a sympathetic listener, he was incapable of being truly down. When things got really sticky and everybody else was depressed, Chris got an extra charge of energy. He actually lit up and set about enjoying any crisis to the fullest. Something about his unquenchable high spirits must have been catching.

The jukebox came on, and I looked up to see which of those wholesome-looking families had put a quarter in to hear heavy metal music. "Oh, my gosh," I gasped. "It's Pete."

A group of guys were standing together by the jukebox, but it was easy for me to spot Pete because he was always the biggest person in any group.

"Don't look at them," Chris warned. "That's the worst thing you can do. Just be casual."

Trying to follow Chris's advice, I took a bite of pizza, but it turned out to be a mistake. I nearly choked.

"Je-rusalem, Andie. Are you okay?"

I coughed and reached for the water glass. "F-fine."

"Well, get a grip, will you? I thought you were glad to be rid of the guy."

"It's not that easy, Chris. I was glad in some ways and kind of sad in others." A cold feeling suddenly gripped the pit of my stomach. "Golly, I just remembered how jealous he was of you. If he sees us, it's going to look like we're out together."

"We are out together."

"I know, but we aren't *really* out together." I stole a look at the boys. "I hope he doesn't come over here. Tell me he's not going to come over here."

"Now you're starting to get me nervous. What exactly do you think he's going to do if he does come over here? Deck me?"

"I don't know. I guess I'm acting stupid."

"Eat your pizza—no, on second thought, don't. I'm not sure I know how to do that Heimlich maneuver stuff. Shake Parmesan on your plate or something. Just try to look natural. Smile." He shook his head. "Jeez, that's awful. You'd better not smile, after all."

"You're getting me all confused."

"I love it when people break up and are just good friends except that they practically have a heart attack every time they see each other."

"You should talk! When I think of all the girls who hate your guts, I'm surprised you aren't afraid to go out."

"Look, Andie, there's no point in making me a nervous wreck just because you are. So far, so good. They're sitting down. I don't think he's seen you."

"That's good." I took a ragged breath. "But how are we going to get up and leave?"

"No problem. We can sit here all night if we have to."

To my horror, I saw that Pete was getting up to go to the salad bar. And the salad bar was right in the middle of the room with a clear view of our booth.

"Don't panic," said Chris in a low voice. "Just remember it takes a lot of concentration to go through a salad bar. All those decisions he has to make. Will it be radishes? Sliced cucumber? Cheese? Mushrooms?

Just don't make any sudden movements. Don't do anything to call attention to yourself."

I threw a suspicious look at Chris. "You're *enjoying* this."

He grinned. "Not true, Andie. My heart bleeds for you."

"Honestly." I slammed my fork down on the table. "You're some kind of ghoul!"

Suddenly there was a huge crash. My eyes snapped to the salad bar, where Pete stood frozen. He looked first at me, then down at the fallen salad plate. Radishes and lettuce were scattered all over the floor, giving new meaning to the words *tossed salad*.

"Lucky thing the plate was plastic," said Chris, grabbing the check off the table. "Let's get out of here."

I jumped up and hurried after Chris. I wiggled my fingers in what I hoped was an approximation of a friendly wave as I passed Pete. He was slowly turning red. If only one of us could have become invisible, I thought wistfully. Chris jerked me ahead.

"Go on outside," Chris instructed me. "I've got to pay." I went outside and stood in the night air shivering until he reappeared.

"How about that!" He grinned at me. "And there are people who'll tell you that this place is dull."

"How can you enjoy something like that, Chris?" I stomped my foot. "You are *sick.*"

"Heck, can't you see it? The drama! The comedy! You've got to admit it's interesting. Lighten up some, Andie."

"It's hard for me to lighten up," I said stiffly, "seeing as how I'm personally involved."

"I guess that might make it hard to see the funny side of it," he allowed. He put his arm around my waist. "Come on, let's get out of here."

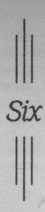

Six

P.J. had to be home right after school, so even though I needed to go to the library after school on Friday, I had to drop him off at home first. "People are going to think I'm some sort of pervert pretty soon," he said bitterly. "I hang around the bathroom talking to anybody who comes in. I'm starved for human companionship, that's what it comes down to."

"You can talk to me."

He shook his head. "It isn't enough, Andie."

"I know you didn't mean that as an insult, so I won't burst into tears."

"It's just that you don't care anything about basketball or baseball. You don't think like a guy."

I didn't bother to deny it. Not only did I not think like a guy, I couldn't understand why anybody would *want* to think like a guy.

"If I couldn't talk to my friends at school, I'd go out of my mind. Lunch is the high point of my day." P.J. sighed. "Too bad that lunch is also the high point of my week. Think of what I'm up against—another weekend of watching Dad's and Ellen's idea of good videocassettes. I'll bet I've seen absolutely every single Laurence Olivier movie ever made."

"He was an awfully good actor, wasn't he?"

P.J. glared at me.

"I have to go to the library now," I explained, "so I'll just drop you off at the house." I pulled the car up into the garage.

"Yeah, I guess I've got to go punch my time clock and put on my ball and chain."

I felt a pang of guilt as I watched P.J. go up the stairs to the kitchen. Would I feel any better if Mom and Richard had grounded me too? I would not, I decided, as I backed the car out of the garage. It would only mean that both P.J. and I would be going crazy instead of just him. It was just a good thing I had gotten my driver's license before the ax fell. If I had still been dependant on P.J. to drive me around, I would have been in a serious mess.

Later that afternoon, when I got back from the library, I found Mom in the kitchen eating an apple. She always said that the smell of apples inspired her and helped her do her plotting.

"Where's P.J.?" I asked. "Still up in his room?"

"He's helping Lupe turn the mattresses. She needed somebody strong to give her a hand, and to my surprise P.J. volunteered."

"He did?" My eyes flickered away from Mom's face. I didn't think that P.J.'s eagerness to help with housework was a good sign.

"I think it'll do him good," said Mom. "To tell you the truth, I'm not sure it's such a good idea to keep a boy as active as P.J. penned up in the house all the time, but Richard was most emphatic about the importance of coming down hard on him. He says P.J. has got to learn self-control and responsibility. If we can't manage that here, maybe a more structured military setting would be better for him." Mom gave a hopeful little smile. "But I think its a good sign that he offered to help with the housework, don't you?"

I didn't answer. "How long do you figure P.J. is going to be grounded, Mom?"

"Two months is what Richard is saying now. Maybe after the first month if he's good, we can loosen up a little bit. Then we'll see."

See what? Whether P.J. is babbling incoherently yet?

I trudged upstairs with my books.

A whooshing thump came from P.J.'s bedroom. When I heard Lupe giggling, I looked in the door. The mattress was lying catty-corner on the box springs. P.J. panting, surveyed it with satisfaction.

I leaned against the doorjamb. *"Qué pasa, P.J.?"*

He turned around. "These suckers are a pain to turn over."

Lupe grabbed one corner of the mattress, and P.J. pushed against the other one until they got it aligned properly over the box springs.

"The really tricky one is going to be the queen-size in Dad and Ellen's room. Keep an ear out, Andie, in case we get trapped under the thing."

Lupe let loose with a torrent of excited Spanish, but I didn't understand what she was saying, and I doubted that P.J. did either. Although after I left I heard him trying a few words in halting Spanish. Maybe Lupe's being around was going to improve his fluency, after all. Mom was probably right about it doing P.J. good to help Lupe around the house. So far it certainly looked more healthy to me than having him sit and brood in his room.

I heard the phone ringing. I knew Mom was back at her computer by now, so I rushed to answer it in my room.

"Hullo?"

"Andie! It's Chris. So how's it going? P.J. putting the moves on the luscious Lupe yet?"

"You've got an evil mind, Chris."

"Me? You were the one who brought it up, remember?"

Actually, it had been P.J.'s idea, I remembered. But so far, I hadn't seen anything going on between them except housework. I was beginning to be surprised at myself for ever having taken P.J. seriously. Boys like to talk big and that was all it amounted to, I decided.

"P.J. is helping Lupe turn mattresses, and I believe he's also practicing his Spanish. It seems to be all perfectly innocent and aboveboard," I said.

"Whoa! That's just when you have to watch out."

"Actually, it's kind of nice the way everything's getting cleaned. Lupe's dusted all the blinds in the house." I noticed that she had just dusted the ones in my room because the slats had been pulled open. I was moving closer to them, admiring what a thorough job she had done when I saw Pete's car drive by. "There goes Pete's car!" I whispered.

"What did you say?"

"Pete! He just drove by outside."

"Andie, I swear, you need help. You can't go in permanent hiding from this guy, you know."

"I don't know why not." I shifted the phone to my other ear. I got so upset when I saw Pete drive by that I had batted my right ear with the telephone. It hurt. "Look, I can't help it if I'm sensitive to the feelings of others. Just because I broke up with Pete doesn't mean I don't care what happens to him. We can't all be carefree and heartless like you."

"I am not heartless."

"I'm sorry, Chris," I said remorsefully. "I didn't mean that. It's just that this stuff with Pete has sort of hit a raw nerve with me."

"Maybe you ought to talk it out with him or something."

"What can I say? There's nothing *to* say. He loves me and I don't love him back."

There was a long silence.

"Chris? Are you still there."

"Sure."

"Would you say something, then? I thought the phone had gone dead."

"I don't know, Andie. It's just a classic rotten situation."

"That's what I've been telling you."

"Quit thinking about it. It's only going to bring you down. Heck, it's bringing *me* down just hearing about it."

"You can't solve every problem just by not thinking about it."

"You're kidding me," he said. "I thought you could."

I ignored his sarcasm. "There's a valuable lesson here," I said. "Don't get involved—that is the lesson. I personally don't plan to fall in love until I'm at least twenty-one. By then I'll be fully mature and able to handle it with complete and total poise. I'll bet you don't catch older people falling apart like this when things don't work out."

Chris whooped. "Hey, don't you read the papers? About how people shoot and stab each other when things don't work out."

"Not reasonable people."

"People in love aren't reasonable people."

"How did you get to be such an authority?" I said.

"I don't know. Forget it. I take it back. I'm not an authority."

"*Now* you've said something," I said with satisfaction. "Anyway, I don't know anybody who's stabbed anybody, and I'll bet you don't either."

"You're right. I'm sorry I said anything."

"Are you feeling okay, Chris?" It wasn't like him to give in so easily in an argument.

"I guess. Maybe. I don't know. I guess I'm feeling kind of low."

"Get out of here! You're not."

Feeling low was not Chris's style. If the world could be divided into problem solvers and problem avoiders, Chris was a born problem-avoider. That was how he stayed so cheerful, I figured.

"I guess I just won't think about it," Chris concluded predictably.

After I hung up, I could hear P.J. in his shower singing "The Midnight Special." He had taken to singing prison songs continually. Last night it had been "Volga Boatmen" as he wiped the dishes. "Yo-yo, heave, ho. Yo-yo, heave, ho," he boomed in a gloomy voice. "Yo-yo, heave, ho. Pull *to*-gether—" It was enough to get on anybody's nerves.

"Will you shut up, P.J.?" yelled Richard. "We're trying to listen to a movie in here."

"More Laurence Olivier, I'll bet," grumbled P.J.

Lupe got off work at five and disappeared into her loft room. It was up to P.J. and me to see to the dinner dishes. That was because Mom was opposed to exploiting the help. Her strong feelings about this were probably rooted in the early days of her widowhood when she worked part-time in bookstores and got exploited herself.

What Lupe did up in her room all that time was anybody's guess. I suspected she listened to the little television Mom had given her and practiced her English.

That night Rachel brought over a care package for

P.J. It was actually very thoughtful. It contained a horror movie video, a copy of *Five Hundred Awesomely Tasteless Jokes,* and some homemade chocolate-chip cookies. "I've been grounded myself," she said sympathetically. "I know how it is. How's he holding up?"

I could hear him upstairs warbling, "If I had the wings of an angel, over these prison walls I would fly."

"Not too good," I said. "This was really sweet of you, Rachel."

"Dooley's going to write him a letter too. It will give him something to read at night when he gets low. Since he can't talk on the phone, I mean."

The front doorbell rang, and I ran to answer it. Pete stood at the front door effectively blocking any view of the outside. I was totally floored. I had been working full-time on avoiding him and now here he was. His brown eyes were cast in shadow by the porch light, giving him a slightly ominous look.

"I'm out of here," said Rachel hastily.

Pete stepped aside to let her pass.

"Andie, we've got to talk," he said.

I looked around for someone to rescue me.

"But—" I said.

P.J. appeared at the head of the stairs. "Pete, old buddy. Did you hear I'm grounded? I'm not allowed to have my friends over, but maybe I could just come on down and we could—"

Richard appeared at the foyer door. "P.J.!" he boomed.

"Look, Dad. It's just Pete. He's not any friend of mine. He's Andie's!"

Richard made a ●peremptory gesture, and P.J. turned abruptly to go back upstairs.

"Hi, there, Pete." Richard wrung his hand. "How are you?"

"I'm fine. How are you, Mr. Grouman?" Pete thrust his hands in his pockets and blushed.

Richard and Mom had been big fans of Pete's. For a second I was afraid Pete would be invited in for a nice long chat, but instead, to my relief, Richard went back to his movie.

"Let's go for a ride," Pete suggested.

"I'm not sure that's a good idea."

"Oh, come on, Andie. You think I'm going to kidnap you or something? Look, if that's the way you feel about it, just forget it." He turned away.

I felt terrible. As close as I had once felt to Pete, it seemed the least I could do. That wasn't too much for him to ask. "Wait. I'm coming! Wait up." I ran to catch up.

I climbed awkwardly into Pete's huge car. All the cars in Pete's family were huge because his entire family was built on a massive scale. It was probably people like them who originally gave rise to the legend of Paul Bunyan.

Getting in, I got the eerie feeling that I was going backward in time. I had gotten in Pete's car so many times when we were going together, and the funny thing was it didn't seem that different getting in right then. It gave me a weird feeling. But everything was different now, I told myself. The feeling I had for Pete was the kind you have for a favorite cousin. Just getting in his car couldn't change that.

Pete switched on the ignition, and the dash lights gave a faint greenish tint to the blunt outlines of his face. He stared rigidly ahead as he pulled out onto the road. "Listen, Andie," he said, "I know I can't compete with Chris."

I started to protest that Chris was just a friend, but then it hit me that if Pete thought I had fallen for Chris, it might save arguing, so I didn't say anything.

"But I thought you said we could still be friends," he went on.

"We are friends," I protested.

"How can we be friends if we never see each other?"

"We see each other in history class."

"You know what I mean, Andie. We never see each other to talk. You're going out of your way to avoid me."

"Oh, no," I said feebly. But it was certainly true that I tried to keep from going near the candy machines at school where I was likely to run into Pete. And I had changed my usual route to my locker.

He looked at me unblinking. "What do you say we go to the game next Friday?" he asked. "Just as friends."

"It wouldn't work out." I could feel my words tumbling over each other. "I'm sorry, Pete, but it just wouldn't."

"Chris is just going to dump you after a while," he said. "He doesn't care about you."

I couldn't believe we were having this ridiculous conversation. "This doesn't have anything to do with Chris," I protested. "I told you—I don't want to be tied down. I need my freedom."

Pete stared ahead again, unseeing. I just hoped he wouldn't steer the car into an oncoming truck. "And Chris doesn't tie you down, huh?"

"I'm not going with Chris!" I cried.

"Heck, it's all over school, Andie. Don't give me that."

"We're just friends."

"Then, I don't see why you and I can't be friends the way you and Chris are friends," he said stubbornly.

"It's not the same thing. You and I were a couple. You can't go back to being regular friends after that. I don't know why, but you just can't."

"I knew it was a mistake to come over," he said bitterly. Abruptly he turned the car around and began driving back up the bluff. The silence in the car was painful.

Why did it have to be this way? I thought miserably. I remembered when I had been desperate to attract Pete's attention. If I happened to catch his eye in class, I got so excited I made a note of it in my diary. In those days I had hung around the candy machine until the sight of a Snickers bar made me feel positively nauseated. We had ended up going together. I vaguely recalled that for a while there I had been delirious with happiness. But it seemed as if in no time I was wondering how I could get free of him. If this was all there was to romance, I thought, it ought to come stamped with a warning label.

Seven

I got an A on my French test. At the top of the page, Madame Vanderwort had scribbled, *"Très bien!"* I could feel elation rising within me, but when I realized what I was allowing to happen I stopped myself. This was no time for overconfidence. With P.J. grounded and Pete lying in wait for me around every corner, things were in a delicate state. I remembered that it had been P.J.'s B on his algebra exam that led him to risk having the party. I didn't want to make a mistake like that.

I had to go to my locker after French to get my algebra book and go to lunch. Since I was taking the long way round to avoid Pete, I was in a dreadful rush. When I saw Suzanne Yelverton, I skidded to a stop so fast I must have left traces of sneaker rubber on the floor. She was standing directly in front of my locker, blocking my way, and she was smiling. Suzanne smiled when things went right—she smiled when things went wrong. The only time I ever saw that smile wiped off her face was when she fell down into a dead faint. Unfortunately, at the moment she was fully conscious.

"Beezie Lewis says you stole Chris away from her," she said.

The only thing that kept me from banging my French book down on her head was knowing that if I did, it would cause talk. "Would you move, Suzanne? I need to get in my locker."

The look on her face reminded me of the people you see gathered around bad car accidents. "So you did, then?" she asked. "It was the way Beezie said?"

"Beezie is out of her mind. Could you please let me get by? I'm running kind of late."

"What's your version of the whole thing? Don't you want to set the record straight?"

It amazed me that she could honestly think I wanted to spill details of my personal life to her. Why, I didn't even *like* her. "Move," I said distinctly. The time for subtlety was past.

She shifted her books to her other hip, as if she were preparing to stand in front of my locker for hours. "You're a very evasive person," she said. "Has anyone ever told you that?"

"I'm very in a hurry. Move, Suzanne, or I'm going to have to move you by force."

To my relief, she stepped aside. It was a good thing because I wasn't actually sure I could have moved her. She was somewhat bigger than I was and solidly built.

However, instead of moving away, the way any sensible person would have, she kept hanging over me. The girl could not take a hint. I flung my locker open and groped blindly for my algebra book. I was doing my best to ignore her, but I kept having an irrational desire to wipe that smile off her face.

"Has Chris dumped you already?" she asked, her beady eyes bright with interest. "Is that why you don't want to talk about it?"

I had an awful feeling that everybody in the locker alcove was listening to what we were saying. "Chris and I are friends," I said. "That's all there is to it. There is no story." I grabbed my algebra book and fled.

I tried to tell myself that Suzanne's problem was that she didn't have a life of her own, but I was so angry that it was hard for me to summon up any charitable thoughts at all.

When I got to lunch later, I looked around for Rachel but didn't see her. She hadn't been in history, either. Obviously, she was out sick, but I couldn't seem to accept that. I needed her. I had been counting on telling her about my bizarre conversation with Suzanne.

Since Rachel wasn't there, I was relieved that P.J. and the gang hadn't got to the cafeteria yet, because I needed a few minutes to pull myself together. Questions of cosmic importance buzzed in my head, like what was Suzanne's problem? And why me, God? I put my tray on an empty table.

Chris pulled up a chair next to me and promptly threw his arm around my shoulders. "What's happening, Andie?"

I froze. "Don't touch me."

"Whah?"

"Chris, if you put your arm around me in the school cafeteria, people are going to think we've got something going."

"What do we care what other people think? You and me are unattached, right? Nothing they say can hurt us."

I saw his point. And yet there seemed to be a flaw in his reasoning somewhere. I thought about it. What would happen if I just let people think that Chris and I were romantically involved? What was the problem with that?

Then it hit me suddenly that if I did that, in only a matter of days people would be coming up to me in the hall to tell me that Chris was fooling around with other girls. Imagining the pity in their eyes, I shuddered.

Chris drew away. "Good grief, Andie. You're getting a thing about this, aren't you?" He raised his hands. "Look, I'm not touching you. Not even a little bit."

"It's just that it sends the wrong signals, Chris. Like, you wouldn't put your arm around Rachel, would you?"

He colored. "That's different. Rachel and I went out one time. People would think—"

"Aha! So you do care what people think."

"Actually, I guess what I care about is what Rachel would think," he admitted. "When you've gone out with somebody, it's tricky to go from that to being friends. I don't know why, but there it is."

I had to agree with that. Who should know about it better than me? Pete's face seemed to swim before my eyes, and I felt faintly sick.

P.J. put his tray down on the table. *"Buenos días!"* He smiled.

"Your accent is improving." Chris shot me a sideways glance. "Do you notice that, Andie?"

"It's because of my hard work, man. Morning, noon, and night I'm working on that Spanish." P.J. smirked. "Señora Carter says she's amazed at the progress I'm making."

Dooley promptly sat down beside P.J.

"Where's Rachel?" I asked.

"She's sick. She's god a code," said Dooley. He whipped out a handkerchief the size of a truce flag and blew his nose.

P.J. snickered. "Catching Rachel's cold, Dooley?"

I moved my chair farther away from Dooley, hoping to escape the shedding viruses. Suddenly I saw myself the way it must look to Suzanne. Here I was, a girl sitting at a lunch table with three boys. Even I had to admit it looked very peculiar. I stole a look around the lunchroom. I saw tables with girls only and tables with boys only and some fully integrated girl-boy tables, but no other table where one girl sat with three boys. Suddenly I felt large and conspicuous. I began to understand how Alice had felt when she nibbled from the wrong side of the mushroom and ended up growing so high her head stuck up through the tree branches.

"What's wrong, Andie?" asked Chris. "You haven't taken a single bite. I thought you liked hot dogs."

"Eat while you can," urged P.J. "Tomorrow we may get mystery meat." He grabbed his throat and made gagging noises.

"You need to put on some weight." Chris pinched my arm, then caught himself. "Oops. I forgot."

"What's going on?" asked P.J.

"Andie doesn't want me to touch her."

"Damn straight," said P.J. "I warned Andie about you."

"Thanks a lot, friend! What do you mean you warned Andie about me?"

"Oh, come on, Chris. You and girls. It's a well-known fact that you're—"

"Notorious," put in Dooley. He sneezed into his napkin.

"Great!" said Chris bitterly. "With friends like you, who needs enemies?" He pushed his chair away and left the table.

"What's with him?" asked Dooley.

"I think you hurt his feelings," I said.

"What did we say?" asked P.J.

"Nothing," said Dooley. "He's just acting weird. It must be something that's going around. Like this blinking code." He sneezed again.

* * *

As soon as I got in from school that afternoon, I took two thousand milligrams of vitamin C and went over to see Rachel. She was in bed, a large wastebasket full of tissues overflowing beside her.

"How are you feeling?" I asked.

"Not so bad." She blew her nose. "There's just one thing that's bothering me." She fixed me with a sorrowful look. "You still think I've got a thing for Chris, don't you?"

I shook my head. "No, absolutely not. I don't, Rachel."

"Because the truth is I wouldn't touch him with a ten-foot pole."

Considering the current state of Rachel's health, I couldn't help thinking that was probably just as well.

"I know Dooley is the only guy for you," I said. "I never thought any different. Honest."

"Well, you're *acting* as if you don't believe me. How do you think it made me feel when Maggie Carter had to call me up and tell me that you were going with Chris?"

I was rocked. "Maggie Carter said I was going with Chris?"

"She said it's all over school." Rachel sniffled. "I'm the last to find out. She says its been going on for weeks, and Chris isn't seeing anybody else, so Maggie says she guesses it must be serious."

"Rachel, don't you think that if I were going with Chris, I would know about it?" I sat down on top of some magazines heaped in a corner. It was a slippery perch, but then it was hard enough to find any place to sit in Rachel's room.

"You mean you're *not* going with him?"

"No! But it's, like, everywhere I turn people are telling me I am. I can't believe it. You know, it's as if they can't understand that a girl and a guy can be friends."

"It's not just that, Andie," Rachel said seriously. "It's Chris's reputation. You know Chris has *always* got a girl. That's just the way he is."

"People change, you know."

"Huh!" snorted Rachel. "Chris change? Good luck."

"I think Chris is getting tired of his reputation." I remembered how he had stalked away from the table at lunch.

"You're falling for him. That's what." Rachel's eyes narrowed.

"Not you too?" I wailed. "Suzanne Yelverton was saying that kind of thing in front of my locker before lunch. The girl is strange. I could hardly even get to my algebra book."

"I refuse to be linked with Suzanne Yelverton in any way whatever," said Rachel. "Let's not get insulting, okay?"

"Then how about you just drop this Chris thing. It's stupid."

"Okay. It's dropped."

"I am not going with him."

"You aren't going with him."

"We are just friends."

"Gotcha. The only thing is you better put out an all-points bulletin or something because it's—"

"All over school," I finished. "I know."

When I left Rachel's house, my head hurt, and my throat didn't feel so great either. When I stepped inside the house, I was startled to hear Lupe giggling. I glanced into the kitchen and saw that P.J. was standing behind Lupe at the kitchen sink, his arms around her. P.J. turned and grinned at me. "I'm showing Lupe how to do the silver polish. The trick is after you polish it, you've got to wash it off." P.J. had obviously been reading the package directions. I had never seen him polishing silver.

Lupe said something in Spanish. To my astonishment, P.J. answered her in Spanish. I couldn't tell what they were saying. I only knew a few Spanish words like chili and tortilla. But I managed to summon up one suitable to the occasion. *"Caramba!"* I exclaimed. I glanced over my shoulder, but there was no sign of Mom. It was a good thing.

"Anything wrong, Andie?" P.J. asked innocently.

"You are going to get in a heap of trouble if you aren't careful," I said. "Believe me."

"Qué?" asked Lupe, looking up at P.J.

"Nothing. *Nada,"* said P.J. "Get out of here, Andie. Can't you see we're busy?"

I went upstairs, gulped down two aspirin, and took more vitamin C, figuring I couldn't be too careful. Then I called Chris.

"P.J. is downstairs with his arms around Lupe."

He whistled. "Fast work."

"He says he's showing her how to polish the silver."

"But you think he's putting the moves on her?"

"I can't honestly believe he has to get that close just to show her how to polish silver. Can't you talk to him, Chris? He doesn't pay a bit of attention to anything I say."

"I don't know, Andie. Preaching's not my thing."

"You want to just stand by and watch P.J. get shipped off to Germany? Is that what you want?"

"No!"

"Then put it to him straight tomorrow at lunch. Maybe he'll listen to you."

"Okay, I'll do my best," said Chris.

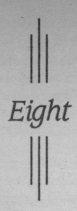

Eight

Rachel was back at school the next day, sniffling disgustingly and wiping her nose. I glanced around at the kids standing in front of the school waiting for the bell to ring. A group of girls looked toward me and then quickly looked away. I wondered what they were saying about me and why they didn't take up a few life-enriching hobbies instead. "If you see Suzanne," I said bitterly, "do me a favor and sneeze on her."

"You shouldn't let her get to you," Rachel said. "My theory is that she's an android. Look at those cold little eyes and that frozen happy-face smile. The girl can't be real."

I only wished that I were the one who was an android. Wouldn't it be terrific if I could program a double of myself every morning and send her off to school while I stayed at home reading? I would miss a lot of pain that way.

Later, in history class, I kept catching Pete staring at me. As soon as the bell rang, unable to take any more of his wistful looks, I hurried out of class.

But as soon as I stepped into the hall, I ran into Alana Jackson. "I just want to say," she said, "that I think you and Chris make a wonderful couple."

"I don't know what you're talking about." I backed away from her. I remembered how upset she had been when she and Chris broke up around Christmas. Her sweetness was totally unconvincing. Suddenly a hulking guy in a leather jacket stepped on my toe and pinioned me in place. Alana, seeing her opportunity, crowded close to me as I winced in pain. "I just hope you know what you're getting into," she said.

"I'm not going with Chris!" I cried. "Can't you grasp that?"

The leather jacket poked me casually in the ribs and moved on to maul others. Alana laid her hand on my arm. "You think I still care about him, don't you?" she said softly. "It's sweet of you to try not to hurt me. But I wouldn't give Chris the time of day. As a matter of fact, I wanted to tell you that I read about his type in psych class—he's a compulsive Romeo. I could photocopy the chapter for you so you could read it. It's very interesting."

"You've got it all wrong, Alana." I was desperate. "Look, I've got to go."

"Off to meet Chris behind the engineering building, huh?" The engineering building, an outbuilding where drafting was taught, was the recognized make-

89

out place at our school. I could feel hot color rushing to my face.

"I'm embarrassing you," Alana said, looking pleased.

"No, no. I've just got to get to class."

Just then Pete came out the door and spotted me. He usually was one of the last out of class. Because he was so big he hated to push people aside. I guess he was afraid he would accidentally plaster them against a wall. His eyes met mine, and for an instant I felt like a deer caught in the headlights of an eighteen-wheeler. "Hi, Andie," he said. His eyes darted from me to Alana. Only seconds before I had been dying to get rid of Alana, but suddenly I felt like grabbing ahold of her and begging her not to leave me. I instinctively felt that when she left, Pete was going to say something we would both regret.

"On your way to French?" he asked me.

I nodded mutely.

"I'll walk with you," he said.

Alana raised her eyebrows expressively. At that point we almost got run down by a trio of sophomores in sweatshirts. A person needed the evasive skills of Joe Montana to avoid getting trampled, and it was fatal to get distracted. People were churning past us on both sides. Since I was boxed in between Pete and Alana, I figured it was only a matter of time before some massive type flattened me.

"Are you okay, Andie?" Pete deflected a couple of guys in letter sweaters who were careening in our direction.

"I'm fine. I'm okay."

"Let's go, then."

I humbly followed in his wake. I had to admit that it was safer getting through the halls with Pete running interference. It was sort of like going to class with a destroyer escort.

As soon as we were out of Alana's earshot, he said it. The thing we would both regret. "I miss you," he said. "Do you miss me just a little?"

"I *like* you, Pete," I said desperately.

"What do you mean by that? I mean, when you say you like me, what kind of like are we talking about here?" He sighed. "Nah, look, forget I said that. I'll just walk you to class, okay?"

I was conscious of attracting stares as we made our way toward Madame Vanderwort's class.

After that I didn't even blink when Madame Vanderwort sprang a pop test on us. It only figured. Not surprisingly, I flunked it.

After school Chris was waiting at the car. "I'm riding with you guys today, remember?"

"Where's P.J.?" I took out my keys.

"Dunno. Guess he'll be along. Hey, three different guys have come up to me to tell me you're cheating on me. What's going on? You and Pete getting back together or what?"

"No, we aren't getting back together! What do you *say* when people give you that stuff?"

"I just look solemn and say, 'I know all about it, but I love her anyway.'"

"Oh, Chris!"

"What's the matter?" Amusement flashed across his face. "Except for Vinnie Leetch. When he told me you were making out with Pete, I told him we had something kinky going and the three of us went out together all the time. I asked him if he'd ever heard of a *ménage à trois*."

I sagged against the car. "You didn't!"

"Yeah, I learned about it from this girl I know who was taking French. It's when instead of being a couple you have a threesome, like in golf. Sounds pretty weird, doesn't it? I mean golf is one thing—" He stopped himself. "Can't see it catching on in this country, can you? Anyway, Vinnie said he always figured you were strange because whenever he saw you in the cafeteria, you were with a bunch of boys." Chris tossed his books in the car, then looked at me in horror. "Good grief, Andie, don't cry! For God's sake. How can you take all that junk seriously? It's just a bunch of stupid jerks talking. Andie?"

I quickly got in behind the wheel, grabbed my purse, and searched desperately for a handkerchief. Chris got in on the other side. "You aren't mad at me, are you?" he asked anxiously. "I just thought it was funny."

Before I knew what I was doing, I had leaned my head against Chris's chest and was letting tears stream down my face. I felt overwhelmed by all the gossip. I seemed to be sinking in it. What had happened to my plan to be a private citizen? I had figured I would be inconspicuous once I shed Pete, who, as I well knew, was about as inconspicuous as a Mack truck. Instead, thanks to Suzanne, I was becoming notorious. I couldn't see how Chris could joke about it.

He touched my cheek with one finger. "Hey, you feel hot. I think you're running a fever."

I sniffled. "Are you serious? Do I really feel feverish?"

"Yeah, what a relief! You really had me going there. For a minute I thought maybe you were letting all this stuff get to you."

"I am! I am!"

P.J. jumped in the backseat. "Hey, don't let me break up anything, you guys."

"I think Andie's got Dooley's cold," Chris said.

"Well, don't go breathing on Chris, will you, Andie? We'll all get it."

"I never get anything," said Chris. "I've got this great immune system."

"Open the windows," said P.J. "Dilute the germs. Hey, you know what I heard? You wouldn't believe this, but it's all over school that Andie—"

"We've heard it," I said wearily. "So shut up, P.J."

"She's running a fever," said Chris. "She doesn't know what she's saying."

"Oh, yes, I do." I wiped my eyes and slowly backed the car out of the parking place. I thought about how famous people must feel when they go through the grocery check-out line and see their names splashed all over the *National Enquirer*. "It's awful to think that perfect strangers are talking about me." I shivered.

"It's just that they don't have anything better to do," said Chris. "You can't let it get to you."

I glanced over at Chris, suddenly conscious of how good he looked. Chris was the problem, I realized with the blinding light of ·revelation. Chris drew gossip even more than Pete because he was so good-looking. If I wanted to avoid people talking about me, I needed to stay away from Chris. It would be pretty lonely, though. I hoped some other solution would occur to me. As I steered out of the parking lot, my head felt light and fuzzy, as if it were full of cotton. It was hard for me to think straight.

When I got home, I went upstairs and climbed into bed. I lay there for some time, trying to read and feeling more and more forlorn. Mom was downstairs in her study and didn't even know that I was sick. P.J. knew but hadn't offered to bring me any hot chicken soup or anything. I was all alone. My only consolation was that the next day I could stay home from school and avoid seeing both Pete and Suzanne Yelverton. That was what made it worthwhile.

I slipped on my bedroom slippers, shuffled to the door, and peeked out into the hall. "P.J.?" I croaked weakly. I seemed to be losing my voice. I was a sick person. It seemed to me that P.J. should go down and get Lupe to fix me some soup.

After a moment I went down the hall and knocked on his door. No answer. I waited for a minute, then opened his door. His bed was neatly made; his waste-basket was empty. I hardly recognized the place, but I remembered that this was not necessarily a sign of anything sinister. Lupe had been cleaning nonstop ever since she began working for us.

I wiped my nose and went downstairs. My mind was not working at top speed. P.J. was probably downstairs, I realized. He was either helping Lupe or stuffing himself in the kitchen or maybe working out on the equipment down in the garage. I should have known that he wouldn't be around when I needed him, because that was the way my day was going. In retrospect, flunking the French quiz seemed almost a bright spot.

When I got downstairs, there was no sign of P.J. I dropped a boullion cube into a cup of water and put it in the microwave. It was so weirdly quiet I could hear the faint hum of the fridge. I opened the kitchen door and peered down into the garage. The light from the high windows in the garage cast a dim illumination over the cars and over P.J.'s exercise equipment, each with a mysterious-looking dial to tell him how fit he was getting. I glanced at the kitchen clock. It was later than I thought, just after five. That meant Lupe would be off work. That was why she wasn't around. But where was P.J.? He wasn't upstairs or downstairs, and he wasn't in the garage. Both cars were present and accounted for, but he could have left the house on foot. It wasn't far to Dooley's house, or to Chris's either. Could he have decided to make a break for it as soon as he noticed Mom was becoming less vigilant?

It wasn't going to be that long until Richard got home. I tiptoed to Mom's study and listened at the door. I could hear the faint hum of the computer and the sound of paper being crumpled up and thrown into the trash. Mom was muttering under her breath. She was obviously having a struggle with her manuscript.

It would be gruesome if Richard came home and found out P.J. had slipped away. I had to cover for him somehow. I knew that. But how? It would be tricky, maybe even impossible.

I took my cup of boullion and went upstairs. If P.J. was sent to Germany, it was his fault, I told myself. I hadn't forced him to have that stupid party, and it hadn't been my idea for him to skip out of the house without permission either. Just the same, maybe I should give Dooley and Chris a call to see if he had shown up there. There still might be time for him to get back home before anybody found out. As I opened the door to my room, I heard a faint giggling in the distance. I paused and listened. That was odd.

I looked up and down the hall but saw no one. At the end of the hall a mirror hung, reflecting the silk flowers Mom had put on a small table. Near the table was the door to the narrow steps that led up to Lupe's room. After a minute I went down the hall, opened the door, and peered up the stairway. The stairs were the one part of the house that had escaped Lupe's cleaning. Dust had gathered at the edges of the steps. Just looking at them made my nose itch. The narrow staircase wound around to a plain door at the top that had been left slightly ajar. "Lupe?" I called, clutching my cup of boullion. Maybe I would ask her if she had seen P.J. But what was the Spanish for "Where has

P.J. gone?" And how could I understand her answer even if I figured out how to ask?

I heard a muffled voice coming from the door. It was not Lupe's.

"P.J.?" Hesitantly I put my foot on the bottom step. What if it wasn't P.J.? What if it was Lupe's boyfriend or someone like that? I was going to be so embarrassed if it was. But if P.J. wasn't up in Lupe's room, then where was he?

The door flew open. P.J. appeared at the top of the stairs. "Andie!" he said. "What are you doing here? You scared the heck out of me."

Lupe peered over his shoulder. Her eyes were dark and frightened.

"I was looking for you," I said. "I've got a cold. I wanted you to get me some hot soup."

"But what—" P.J. glanced around at Lupe. "Oh, never mind. I gotta go, Lupe. *Adios.*" He galloped down the stairs.

I waited until we had gotten out of Lupe's hearing before I exploded. "P.J., are you out of your mind? You don't have any business up in Lupe's room. Mom and Richard would have a fit! You must have totally taken leave of your senses."

"Come on, Andie, cool it. It's pretty lonely for Lupe up there with nothing but that dinky little television your mom gave her. She doesn't know anybody in town. Think about it."

"She can go out and meet people. Nobody's stopping her. She could join a church, go to the mall, go see a movie, so don't give me that."

P.J. cast a glance behind us. "She doesn't like to go out. You know how shy she is. She jumps every time she sees a shadow. It's pathetic."

"It's not up to you to bring sunshine into her life, P.J. I promise you, you are going to end up in so much trouble it's going to make that stuff about the party look like a day at the beach. I wish that just once you'd listen to me."

"Did you know your eyes are kind of glazed over? I better go get you an aspirin."

Undeniably, I did feel a tad wobbly. I went on into my room and fell into the bed. A few minutes later P.J. came upstairs with a tray. He had brought me aspirin, orange juice, crackers, and chicken-noodle soup. Tears welled up in my eyes. I was a regular waterworks lately. I supposed it was the fever. "This is so sweet of you, P.J."

"De nada," he said airily.

"P.J., *promise* me that you aren't going to go up to Lupe's room anymore. What's it going to be like for me if you get shipped off to Germany? Have you thought of that? I'll be all alone in this big house with nobody at all to yell at."

"You worry too much!" He quickly ducked out of the room. I noticed he hadn't made any promises.

After I swallowed the two aspirin, I told myself I felt better. Maybe it was the•placebo effect, but who cared? I dialed Chris and filled him in on the latest development.

"This is very bad," I told him. "What if I hadn't

gone looking for P.J.? What if Richard had come home and not been able to find him?" I shuddered. "Either I'm getting an awful premonition, Chris, or else I'm getting chills and fever."

"Take some aspirin."

"I have!"

"Don't panic. I've got an idea."

"You didn't say anything to P.J. at lunch, did you? And you promised you'd talk to him."

"It wouldn't do any good. Listen, I've got a better idea."

"This better be good."

"We'll write him anonymous letters."

"What did you say?"

"We'll write him threatening letters. We'll pretend they come from Lupe's boyfriend. I can see the whole thing now. Lupe's boyfriend is this tall, dark type, very macho, and he keeps testing his knife against his thumb."

"You've seen too many movies, Chris."

"So what? P.J.'s seen the same movies. Besides, it doesn't have to be all that convincing. Just enough to make P.J. feel guilty.

I remembered how jumpy P.J. had been after the big party. Chris was right. Underneath that facade of impenetrable cool, P.J. did have a conscience that we could work on.

"He's got to be worried already," said Chris. "All we need to do is give his conscience a little nudge."

"Baybe you're ride." I reached for the box of tissue

and blew my nose. "It's worth a try. You do it, Chris. Be sure to disguise your handwriting."

"I thought I'd type it."

"I don't think the kind of guy who carries a knife knows how to type."

"I'll iron out the details," he said airily. "Don't give it another thought. I'll take care of the whole thing."

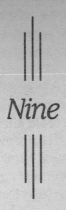

Nine

I spent three happy days at home. Except for the fact that my head hurt, my nose hurt, and I could hardly talk or breathe, it was wonderful. I might have spent a vast amount of time soaking in a hot tub and sniffing nasal spray, but at least I didn't have to cope with Suzanne Yelverton. It seemed like a fair trade-off.

Mom came in and sat at the foot of my bed. "How are you feeling, sweetheart?"

I eyed her cautiously over the handkerchief wadded in my hand. "Better," I admitted.

"Don't you think you'd better give some thought to getting back to school? You aren't running a fever now, and you must be getting awfully far behind in your work."

I thought of Suzanne, Pete, and Alana and suddenly felt rather ill. "I don't know if I'm quite up to it yet, Mom. I don't want to have a relapse."

"Maybe we'd better get you in to see a doctor. Can you breathe all right? You don't think you could be coming down with pneumonia, do you?" Her eyes widened anxiously.

I could tell that her imagination was switching into high gear. Before she could ask me if my toenails felt soft and if I'd ever considered that I might have beriberi, I hastily assured her that I was sure I would be ready to go back the next day.

"Oh, good." She relaxed. "Do you want me to bring you anything?"

"No, thanks. P.J. just brought me all this orange juice and coffee cake." Actually, P.J. had been so good about waiting on me since I got sick that it made me positively suspicious. Was he deliberately trying to keep me in my room so I wouldn't find him and Lupe in compromising situations? I wished that Chris had hand-delivered his threatening letter instead of sending it through the U.S. mail. Waiting for it was killing me.

"P.J. is being so sweet," Mom said. "I have to admit that Richard and I have been pleasantly surprised at how well he's taken being grounded. He seems perfectly happy to putter around here helping Lupe with the housework." Mom's auburn hair stood out around her face like an aureole, framing her pale face and her trusting eyes. "It almost makes me wonder if he wasn't relieved to have limits set. You know, not everybody has your self-discipline, Andie. Some kids need firm rules. His Spanish grades have improved

102

beyond our wildest imaginings. I personally wouldn't be surprised if he was secretly glad to have an excuse to sit home and apply himself."

"Mmmph," I said enigmatically, burying my nose in my handkerchief.

"What did you say?"

"I said, 'You may be right.'" Or you may be wrong, I thought. More likely the latter.

Mom stood up. "Well, I'd better let you get some rest."

"No, no! I'm up," I said, throwing off the covers. "In fact, maybe I'll just run downstairs and check the mail."

"Take it easy, darling. You don't want to overdo just at first."

"I think I need to get up and move around some." I jumped out of bed.

"Well, if you think so," said Mom.

Being young and fast on my feet, I beat Mom downstairs. I was relieved to see that Lupe was vacuuming the living room and that P.J. was in the kitchen eating a peanut butter sandwich. Nothing very compromising about that.

"I'm going out to check the mail," I said.

"I thought you were dying from that stupid cold of yours," said P.J.

"That was yesterday. Today I'm fine." I pulled my bathrobe tightly around me, dashed outside, and made a quick run down the driveway to the mailbox. It was stuffed with junk mail. As I walked back to the house, I leafed through the circulars and bills. There it was—a square envelope for P. J. Grouman with no return address. I smiled, but then forced myself to assume an expression of unconcern. When I went back in the house, the vacuum was still roaring in the living room. I went into the kitchen and tossed the envelope onto the kitchen counter in front of P.J. "Something for you," I said.

"You sure?" He frowned. "I hardly ever get any mail." He reached for the envelope, puzzled.

I poured myself some fresh orange juice and watched him out of the corner of my eye. "Anything interesting?"

He dropped the envelope. Then he thought better of it, picked it up again, folded it carefully, and stuck it in the pocket of his jeans. "Nope. It's not from anybody you know."

I noticed P.J. was a little pale, but I couldn't ask him any more questions without giving myself away.

When Chris got in the car on Monday morning, I grinned and circled my thumb and middle finger in an okay sign. P.J. didn't notice. He was staring at the road ahead with a vacant expression. I supposed he was pondering the threats made in Chris's letter.

"Good to see you on your feet again, Andie." Chris slid in the front seat next to P.J. "Ready for that algebra test, man?"

"What?" P.J. looked at Chris blankly.

"The algebra test? Hey, we are going to school, aren't we?"

"Sure," P.J. said irritably. He stepped on the accelerator so fast our heads snapped back.

"How's that whiplash, Andie?" Chris asked, rubbing the back of his neck. "I think I'll recover in time."

"You wanted me to get a move on, didn't you?" snapped P.J. "All you guys do is complain."

"Sorry." Chris winked at me.

I sighed contentedly. At last everything was going just according to plan.

When we got to school, P.J. pulled into the parking lot and got out of the car without saying a word. "Has he said anything about the letter?" whispered Chris.

"Not a word," I whispered.

"Are you two going to take all day?" P.J. yelled. "Get out of the car. I want to lock up."

I stepped out of the car only to find myself standing eyeball to eyeball with Suzanne Yelverton. Smiling, she looked at Chris, then at me, then at the car.

Okay, so maybe not exactly *everything* was going according to plan.

That next Wednesday Chris made it to lunch before anyone else. "Got out of **algebra** early to help Mrs. Myer with the projector," he explained. He plopped his tray down on the table, next to mine. "This is good because I need you to help me with another letter."

I quickly glanced around the cafeteria, but so far there was no sign of P.J. It seemed safe to continue. "Okay, shoot."

"I think we need to play on his paranoia. What do

you think? The theme should be something along the lines of 'every breath you take, every step you make I'm watching you.' But exactly how do I put it? Give me some words I can use. You're good at this kind of thing."

"How about 'Don't think you can fool me. I saw you two together.'"

"That's good." Chris made a note on his napkin, "Except that instead of 'saw', we'll put 'I *see* you and Lupe together.' We don't want to sound too literate. Literate people always sound as if you can reason with them. The effect we're after here is cold fear. What do you think of 'You die, pig,' as a complimentary conclusion?"

"Kind of blunt, isn't it? I mean, where do we go from there?"

"We put a drop of blood next to the signature?"

"What would that show? That Carlos cut himself shaving?"

"He's always testing his knife against his thumb. Remember?"

"I can't believe P.J. is going to swallow this, Chris. It's so unreal."

"Did you see his face this morning? Don't argue with success."

Chris was right. It did seem that P.J. was buying Carlos the Cutthroat hook, line, and sinker, at least if his pallor that morning was any sign.

"Watch out," said Chris. "Here he comes." He stashed the napkin in his pocket.

"How'd you get out of algebra, Chris?" P.J. put his tray down abruptly and all the silverware rattled. "What's your secret?"

"Had to help Mrs. Myer with the projector," Chris said. "You, too, could have this privilege if you belonged to the projector club. Where's Dooley?"

"He and Rachel brought sandwiches and are eating behind the engineering building," P.J. said. "That's what I hate about the weather warming up. Everywhere you look you see somebody making out." This observation must have started a gloomy train of thought because he then stared disconsolately at his mystery meat without making a single crack about it.

"You'll be glad later that you're not into that," I assured him. "When all those couples are breaking up and miserable."

"Who says I'm not into that?" he protested. But then he looked as if he regretted saying anything and slipped down a little in his seat. If he had had a thought balloon drawn above his head, it couldn't have been more obvious that he was thinking about the letter he had gotten.

"Don't pay any attention to Andie," Chris said. "She's kind of phobic about this love thing."

"What about you?" I said indignantly. "I don't notice you rushing into anything lately."

"That's different."

"How is it different? Oh, I get it. You mean it's different because you've already been out with every girl in school?"

"Not a bit. That's not what I'm getting at. What I'm saying is that you don't have anything to be phobic about, Andie. When it comes to going out, it's the guy who takes all the risks."

"He's right," said P.J., resting his forehead on his hand and looking sick. Anybody might have guessed he had actually eaten the mystery meat.

"Are you okay, P.J.?" I asked. "No fever or anything?"

"I'm fine," he said shortly.

I turned back to Chris. "How can you sit there and say the boy takes all the risks after what I've gone through with Pete!"

Chris waved that away. "What I'm saying is that usually it's the guy that does the asking. He's the one that has to face somebody laughing in his face."

"Sure, Chris. Tell us about all your rejection."

"It's just Chris's idea of sick humor," said P.J. "He doesn't have any idea what *real* trouble is."

"Okay, there are ways to minimize the problem," Chris admitted. "Like you can just ask out girls you're sure of, girls who like you."

"How can you tell when girls like you?" I asked.

"There are hundreds of ways. You just know."

"Do they live and breathe?" asked P.J. sourly. "That's what it comes down to in Chris's case."

"Don't give me that," said Chris. "I've been turned down."

"You've been turned down?" My eyes widened. "We want to know, Chris. Tell us more. Give us the gruesome details."

"Look, I'd rather not think about it, if you don't mind. It kind of brings me down."

"Name names," I insisted.

"Well, Cassie Marks, for one."

"Cassie Marks!" P.J. sneered. "She's been going with Michael Jamison since the seventh grade. What made you ask Cassie Marks?"

"I dunno. I must be stupid or something."

"That just proves our point, man. Nobody but you would even think of asking out Cassie Marks."

"I just don't see that you've got anything to complain about," I said. "Look at it rationally. Even if you just limited yourself to girls who obviously like you, you'd still have lots to choose from."

"It's not that easy."

"But I thought you said you could always tell if they liked you."

"Sure. In most cases. But there can be complicating factors."

"Like if you've got a language barrier," put in P.J. glumly.

"Right. Or like if you're good friends. I mean, you might know a girl likes you, but you can't figure out if she likes you that way."

"I'm glad I'm not a boy." I pressed a hole in my mashed potatoes, put a pat of butter in it, and watched as it refused to melt. "It's bad enough being a girl."

Chris grinned. "You don't want to be a boy, you don't want to be a girl. What do you have in mind?"

"I want to be an android," I said firmly. "I've got it all figured out. No pain."

"Oh, my gosh," said Chris. "Don't look now, but Pete just came in."

"Crawl under the table, Andie," said P.J.

"Wait a minute," said Chris. "It's all right. He's got a girl with him."

"A girl!" I swiveled around in my seat and stared. Sure enough, a girl was smiling up at Pete. There was a silly expression on his face that gave me a sharp pain in my stomach. Looking ridiculously happy, they made their way through the crowd at the door.

"Maybe he's trying to make you jealous," suggested P.J.

I looked down at my plate and cut my meat into squares. Then I cut them into tinier squares. If I kept it up, I would have mystery meat broken down into its basic chemical components, which could be a real breakthrough. Then we would know for sure what was in the stuff.

"Are you okay, Andie?" Chris asked.

"Of course. I am very happy that Pete has found someone who appreciates him."

"Good," said Chris.

I stabbed a piece of meat with a fork. "But he sure didn't waste any time, did he?"

Nobody said anything. I wanted P.J. to make one of his dumb jokes, but instead a sympathetic silence fell over the table. That was extremely hard to take.

I lifted my fork to my mouth.

"Do us a favor and don't eat that," Chris said. "You're only going to choke on it."

I lowered my fork. "If you think I am upset about Pete finding somebody else," I said, "you are totally mistaken." I looked down at my plate and sighed. "It's just that if I were an android, my life would be so much simpler."

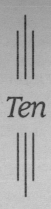

Ten

I surprised myself by minding rather a lot that Pete had found someone new. These affairs of the heart were more complicated than I had imagined. It seemed that I could not want someone and yet still not want anyone else to have him. It was a very humbling thought. I was forced to conclude that I was not as nice a person as I had thought.

"Oops," Mom said a week later as she was taking dinner rolls out of the freezer. "I think we may be out of butter." She opened the refrigerator, then glanced over at P.J. He was in the family room doing his Spanish homework. Judging from the anxious look on P.J.'s face, I judged he was busy looking for the Spanish equivalent of "Please don't kill me."

"P.J." said Mom, "why don't you go down to the store for me and get some butter?"

It had been a full month since P.J. had been

grounded. I suppose Mom and Richard had decided to relax their grip a little.

P.J. didn't look up from his Spanish book. "Andie can do it. Can't you, Andie?"

"You don't want to go out to the store?" Mom was amazed. "You wouldn't have to come right back, you understand. You could stop off and get yourself an ice-cream cone as long as it only took a minute or two."

"I think I'll pass," P.J. said. "Andie can do it."

I followed Mom into her study to get money out of her purse. "I'm worried about that boy," she said. "I thought he'd jump at the chance to get out of the house."

"I guess he's busy studying," I said.

With the key ring dangling from my little finger, I peeked in the family room. P.J.'s head was still bent over his book. Lamplight streamed down on his dark hair. "You sure you don't want to come along?" I asked him.

"Nope. You go," he said.

I could see why Mom thought P.J. was acting peculiar. You would expect that after a whole month of being held prisoner, he would be excited to get out of the house for any reason whatsoever. I just hoped his unusual behavior wasn't going to cause Mom to start asking awkward questions.

After I got back from the convenience store, I went up to my room, thinking I would give Chris a call. To my surprise, P.J. came in and closed the door behind

113

him. "Andie, I need to talk." He pulled my blinds shut. I gave him a startled look.

"I think somebody may be following me," he said.

I was careful to look surprised. I didn't want him to suspect that I knew what was wrong. "Why would anybody be following you?"

"Just take it from me, someone is. Did you know that Lupe has a boyfriend?"

"No. How can she? She hardly ever goes out. I just don't see how she can have a boyfriend. Where would she meet him?"

"That's kinda what I thought. When I asked her about it, she denied it, but I don't believe her. I swear I've never seen anybody look so guilty. And this is the thing, Andie." His eyes opened wide. "He's after me."

"Hold it. Are you saying Lupe's boyfriend is after you? That doesn't make sense."

"Maybe not, but it's true. I've been getting these letters. Threatening letters." He gulped. "I tell you, every day I run out to the mailbox in a sweat, worried that Ellen or somebody is going to get there first and see one of those things. They're always just on notebook paper and they are definitely creepy. Can you see me explaining to Dad how some crazy guy with a knife between his teeth happens to be trailing me?"

"Oh, I wouldn't tell Richard about it," I said.

"Yeah, but this is no joke. I tell you, it isn't just the letters. He's following me. Like, he knows we stop for gas over on MacDugal Street. How would anybody know that unless he was following me?"

"It might be a lucky guess."

"Yeah, sure," he said disdainfully. "You don't think Lupe's been blowing things up between me and her trying to make this guy jealous or something? I mean"—he glanced at the window—"between you and me this guy sounds dangerous."

"Golly! Really?" I was beginning to wonder if Chris had overdone the threats slightly.

"Yeah." P.J. ran his finger inside his collar. "I mean, if she was trying to make him jealous, she sure as heck did. Got any ideas?"

"I don't know, P.J. The only thing I can suggest is to stay away from Lupe."

"I *have* been staying away!" he cried. "I mean, there was never anything between us. Nothing." He hesitated. "Maybe I flirted a little bit, but I never got anywhere." He parted the blinds with his fingers and peered outside. "You don't think somebody could be watching the house, do you? Look at that delivery van across the street. 'Balloons Are Us'? Who is he kidding? I've seen that exact kind of van in a million spy movies."

"Rachel says the Masons are having a big party."

"If I hear a peep from that party"—P.J. cracked a wobbly smile—"I'm calling the cops." The smile faded from his face. "I'd love to see a cop about now. I never thought I'd hear myself say that."

"I just don't see how anybody could be following you. Don't you think it's very possible you're just getting a tiny bit crazy on account of being grounded so long?"

"But what about the letters?" He smacked his hand

115

down on the dresser. "I've got the threats in black and white. I'm not making this stuff up."

"I didn't say you were!"

"I'd show you some of them, but I figured I'd better destroy them." He shuddered. "Imagine if Dad found one. He'd never believe I hadn't done anything to deserve it."

"But maybe since you've quit hitting on Lupe the letters will stop."

"You *do* think the guy is watching me, then! You must think that if you think he'll know I've quit messing with Lupe."

"Well, no—"

"Then how's he going to know what I do?"

"I don't know," I said lamely.

"Let me tell you, Andie. This is beyond funny. There's a crazy guy out there who's stalking me."

"Maybe it's not as bad as that," I said.

"Easy for you to say," said P.J. bitterly.

There was a knock on my door. We both jumped a mile. "Who is it?" I called.

Mom pushed the door open. She was obviously surprised to see P.J. in my room. I knew I should have made up some excuse, but I couldn't think of anything, so P.J. and I just stood there looking like certified•co-conspirators. As she looked back and forth from me to P.J., I smiled weakly.

After a minute she seemed to lose interest in us. Obviously something more pressing was on her mind. She sat down at my dressing table. "Lupe just tried to hand in her resignation." It was pretty clear to me that

Mom didn't have a clue as to what was going on, and I was glad about that, anyway. "I do think," Mom said, "I got the gist of what she was trying to tell me. But, of course, I was leafing through the Spanish-English dictionary like mad. Do you kids know anything about this?"

"No!" we exclaimed in chorus.

"You are being nice to Lupe, aren't you?" asked Mom.

P.J. was obviously unable to commit himself. I suppose he was afraid Lupe's boyfriend might have electronic surveillance equipment trained on the house to pick up his every word. "Well—" he hedged.

"Sure, we're nice to her," I put in. "I guess what P.J. means is we hardly have anything to do with her, Mom. She's always working, and after all, we've got our own lives, right, P.J.?"

"Absolutely!" He exchanged a frightened glance with me.

Mom was thoughtful. "I have the impression you two were not too happy about having to keep the house neat, and I honestly can understand that. It's a big change for us all. But Richard really likes the house neat. If Lupe left we'd only have to get someone else, and it wouldn't be easy to find anyone as good."

"Oh, absolutely," I echoed.

P.J. shot me a guilty look, but luckily Mom didn't see it. "I just can't understand why she suddenly wants to leave," Mom said. "She seemed fine until today. She never complained before."

"It can't have anything to do with us," I said.

"Is that what you'd say too, P.J.?" Mom watched him closely.

"Sure. Right! I agree with Andie."

Mom stood up. "Well, the crisis is averted for the moment, at least. I've given her a raise, and she says she'll stay for now. I just wanted to tell you about it so you could both make an extra effort to be considerate of her."

"You can count on us, Mom," I said.

Mom gave us a quizzical look but didn't ask any more questions. When she at last withdrew, she left my door ajar.

P.J. muttered, "Sure, I'll try being nice to Lupe. Sure, and Lupe's boyfriend will cut off my ear, maybe." He heaved a sigh. "I know this makes no sense, Andie, but I do feel better since I've told you about it. I mean, if my body is found floating facedown, at least I know that you'll tell the cops they should be looking for Lupe's boyfriend." He smiled a crooked grin. "Jeez, I wish I could talk to Chris and Dooley about this. They could be my bodyguards. But I tell you, this is not something I feel like bringing up in the school cafeteria. Why don't you fill them in on everything for me? In a general way, I mean. Let them know that if anybody asks where I am, they don't know me and they haven't seen me."

"Sure. I will, but don't worry. Something tells me it's going to work out all right."

"Sure." He winced. "That's what people always say when it's not their problem."

As soon as P.J. left, I called Chris. "We've got to talk," I said. "I'll come by your house and get you."

One thing I was clear about was that I didn't want to risk Mom or P.J. picking up the extension while I was talking to Chris.

I grabbed the car keys and headed downstairs. Mom was in the kitchen taking out the casserole Lupe had made.

"I'm going out for burgers with Chris, Mom. Don't hold supper for me."

"You certainly are seeing a lot of Chris these days."

"I always see a lot of Chris, Mom. We're good buddies."

Mom had trouble grasping that. The concept of "buddies" did not feature largely in her fictional world, which consisted largely of powerful men with dark souls, who lost no time sweeping women off their feet and away to some castle.

Come to think of it, Mom's own life had run sort of along those standard romantic lines. My father had been a race car driver before he had died suddenly in a fiery crash, leaving her a young struggling widow. And Richard, owner of Grouman's Department Stores, was close enough to Mom's idea of a prince, if not mine. I suppose she felt he had swept her off to his three-story, ranch-style castle with its three-car garage.

But I was different from Mom. I had no intention of living my life in the pink haze of romance, and I was not the type to be swept off my feet. I was into reality.

119

I had been successfully steering my way clear of romance ever since New Year's, and I was the better for it. Whenever I thought of what a pickle P.J. had landed himself in by chasing girls, I shuddered. If it hadn't been for my timely intervention, he might have been on his way to Germany right now. And then there was Chris. Some might call him a connoisseur of romance, but he certainly hadn't found it smooth sailing. And then there was the most important example—me. I'd had a terrible time breaking up with Pete. It might not be a scientifically selected sample, but it was enough to convince me. What I needed was not romance, but space.

When I got to Chris's house, his younger brothers were running around the yard. A bunch of other kids were there, too, and they were all yelling. Even in the dusk I could tell Chris's brothers from the others because they were so blond. One of them jumped up on Chris's back as he came out the door. "Down, squirt," said Chris.

"Chris 'n' Andie, sitting in a tree, k-i-s-s-i-n-g," sang the kid.

Chris pried his brother off his back and got in my car. "Too bad my folks didn't stop with me," he said. "They didn't know enough to quit while they were ahead."

I backed the car out of the driveway, going carefully so as not to flatten any of Chris's little brothers or their playmates. "Chris, what exactly did you *say* to P.J. in that last letter?"

"It was good, if I do say so myself. Kind of sinister

but in a subtle way. It started out, 'I see you drive to school at eight-ten A.M. You have no secrets. I see you get gas at MacDugal Street. You cannot escape me.' Those may not be my exact words, but close enough. I figured that would give him the idea that somebody really was watching him."

"Well, it worked. Today P.J. was afraid to go out to the convenience store to get butter for Mom."

Chris whooped. "That's great. But I'm not finished yet. I've got something even better coming up. I've already talked to Tommy Driggers. I'm going to borrow Tommy's van and drive back and forth in front of your house, maybe wearing a black wig. What do you think? Neat, huh?"

"Scratch the whole idea," I said. "Don't you hear what I'm saying? P.J. is freaking out. He doesn't even go *near* Lupe anymore. He's a quivering mass of nerves. He was in my room a few minutes ago telling me the whole story, which is not a bit like him. Also there have already been some serious repercussions. Lupe almost quit this afternoon. I think it's because P.J. got mad at her and accused her of having a crazy boyfriend. Now Mom is having a fit. She made us swear we wouldn't get Lupe upset ever again."

"Gee, this is even better than we figured." Chris was impressed. "Who'd have believed that P.J. would swallow it like that?"

"It's pathetic, Chris. He's really scared."

"Okay, I guess I did overdo it." He looked crestfallen. "I didn't mean for him to have a heart attack or anything."

"And have you thought of this?" I lowered my voice. "If he gets scared enough, he's going to tell Richard all about it and ask for protection."

"You really think he'd do that?"

"What would you do if you thought a homicidal maniac was stalking you?"

"I guess you're right."

"I just hope we haven't done P.J. any permanent damage. The way things are going he may need extensive therapy before he's willing to even go outside again."

"He'll get over it." Chris grinned. "And we've already done what we had to do. Mission accomplished, partner." He put his arm around me and squeezed. I cringed a little. It wasn't that I minded Chris's having his arm around me. Chris was naturally warm and affectionate, and I liked being close to him. It was just that I halfway expected Suzanne Yelverton to pop out from behind the nearest house with witnesses and ask me to sign on the dotted line that Chris and I were going together. As a matter of fact, since my experience with Suzanne, I could sort of identify with how P.J. felt about being stalked.

We drove to the burger place and went in. Chris got one of those double-decker hamburgers with special sauce, the kind that by rights ought to come with both a health warning and a bib. I ordered a somewhat smaller, tidier burger.

"Look, there's no serious harm done, Andie," Chris said. "P.J.'s tougher than he looks. So how about a smile, huh?"

"I'll work on it." I unwrapped my burger. "There's just one thing." I felt silly but I decided to say it anyway. "Could you possibly stop your brothers from singing that dumb song when I drive up?" Already I found myself dreading the chorus of "Andie and Chris sitting in a tree" that would meet me when we got back to Chris's house.

"I can tell you don't have any little brothers. No, I can't stop them. Why does it get to you so much?"

"I don't know." I opened my hamburger and rearranged the pickles. I like my pickles spread out, not overlapping. I like a lot of things different from the way they are, but pickles are among the few things in my life that I am able to fix. "I could just as easily ask why it doesn't get to you," I said.

He shrugged. "I'm hardened. I remember one time the little creeps really got to me. I mean big time. I went straight for their throats. I had hold of Jeff and was shaking him when Dad came out and made me drop him. When Dad heard the whole story, he was on my side, but he said I did *not* have his permission to murder Jeff no matter what he did. I guess that was a turning point for me. I don't know, I just finally realized that I had to learn to live with them, that's all. I try not to let them get to me. It ought to be easy for you. You don't have to put up with them at breakfast." He looked at me curiously. "What's the big deal?"

I didn't know. All I knew was that I felt unbearably self-conscious. I bit into my hamburger and tried to think of something entirely different—French verbs, political changes in Eastern Europe. Nothing worked.

I had to remind myself to blink, to chew, to look natural. I couldn't remember what I normally did with my hands, and I held on to that hamburger as if it were a life raft.

Chris pulled out his wallet and began leafing through his various video membership cards. It looked as if he belonged to fifteen or twenty video clubs. Finally he came on a small newspaper clipping and laid it on the table. "Take a look at this."

It said, "Lambada at the Y. Learn the exotic dance of love. Only $25 with Y membership, $35 without membership."

"What do you think?" he asked. "I called about it and it turns out you've got to have a partner to take the class. Want to do it?"

"I don't know, Chris. I never really got beyond the two-step. You really ought to ask somebody who's more into dancing."

"Come on," he said. "There isn't anybody else I can ask. You won't do it?"

I shook my head. He shuffled his video cards together again, tucked the newspaper clipping under them, and put them back in his wallet.

"What happened to all those girls of yours?" I asked. "Why don't you ask one of them?"

He looked annoyed. "I told you that flagging down a new one every weekend was getting to me, didn't I?"

"So—"

"So, I've given up girls."

That was the point at which I would normally have made some smart remark, but a novel and uncomfortable idea buzzing around in my brain kept me from saying anything. Was it remotely possible that I was going with Chris and that I didn't even realize it?

I pulled myself together. It wasn't possible. I was definitely losing it.

Chris was sitting inches away from me, looking so good he could have been the prize in the Cracker Jack box. He was practically my best friend. I expected him to help me out when I got in a mess. I cried on his shoulder, I•filched french fries off his plate, and I really liked him. I decided to come right out and say what was on my mind.

"Chris, you don't think it's possible that you and I could be going together without realizing it."

He tilted his head and narrowed his eyes until they were merry slits of blue. "Nah," he said. "I mean, being as how you don't want to get involved and I don't want to get involved, I don't see how we could possibly be going together, do you?"

I put down my burger. "You can't imagine how much better that makes me feel. I had this awfully funny feeling there for a minute. It's hard to explain—"

"Give it a try." He leaned toward me. "I'm interested."

"I just really like to be in control, you know. It's very important to me. I would hate to think that things were going on without my realizing it. I mean, think of it. If I could be going with somebody without realizing it, where would it end? I could end up married or converted to a new religion or something and still not have a clue. The whole idea is indescribably creepy."

He grinned. "You're panicking, Andie. You better take a deep breath or something."

I realized that Chris was right. I had come slightly unglued. I was fast regretting that I had said anything. "I haven't embarrassed you, have I?"

"Nah. We've got a good thing going, right?"

"Right. I agree. We've got a good thing."

"So, no problem, right?"

"Right."

I just sat there, as the *rights* flew fast and furiously between us, and by imperceptible degrees I began to feel better. Nothing was any different from how it had always been. There was no reason for me to be getting weird about Chris. This was all Suzanne Yelverton's fault. She was having a very strange effect on my mind.

After we finished eating, I drove Chris home. Chris's parents had turned on the floodlights in the front yard, obviously a last-ditch effort to keep the kids playing outside as long as possible. One kid was roped to the oak on the front lawn, and the others were running around him in a circle screaming. I personally would not have cared to be the kid who was tied up. Those kids looked like blood-thirsty little devils to me.

Chris threw open the door on his side, and the two blond kids ran over to the car shrieking, "Chris and Andie, sitting in a tree, k-i-s-s-i-n-g."

Chris slid back across the seat and closed the door. "I think we ought to teach those brats a lesson."

"You can't kill them," I reminded him regretfully.

"Nope," he said. Suddenly he bent his head close to mine and kissed me on the lips. I felt his fingers pressing cool at the back of my neck for a second, and the most amazing sense of peace filtered through me. It was like leaves drifting down. I lost all sense of time. It was very strange.

I was vaguely conscious of shrieks and of small bodies flailing against the car. Chris looked around momentarily to check our audience and then smiled and kissed me again.

I wasn't sure how I felt about it, but the kids surrounding the car thought it was the most shocking thing since Disney started putting out R-rated movies. They were going "Woo-oo," and shrieking with the kind of decibels that induce ear damage.

Chris's lips brushed softly against mine and lingered there. When he finally drew away from me, I shook my hair back in place and took a few deep breaths. "Is this part of some grand plan of yours or something?" I asked uneasily. "I mean is there some particular reason you're kissing me like that?"

"Sure. My idea is that if we kiss like this every time we pull up in front of the house, eventually they'll get bored with the whole thing. Right?"

I looked around me at the avid little faces pressing their noses against the car windows. "I wouldn't hold my breath," I said.

Chris punched me gently. "See ya," he said. "And don't run over any of them when you're backing out. I mean, they may get on our nerves, but a couple of them are my blood relatives."

I backed out of the driveway, very carefully. My mind was in such a state of some confusion I was afraid I was going to drive into a tree.

I had the impulse to go over to Rachel's and tell her about what had happened. But I could almost hear her voice already. "You're falling for him, aren't you? I can tell." There is a certain disadvantage in knowing a friend so well you can predict what they will say. You may just decide you don't want to hear it.

So, instead of going next door to Rachel's, I went home. Mom and Richard were in the family room watching the evening news. I went upstairs and tapped on P.J.'s door.

"I need to talk," I said when he opened it.

"Have a seat." He gestured broadly. "Thanks to Lupe's cleaning, you can sit absolutely anywhere. Everything's clean. Everything's cleared off." His face darkened. "We were a lot better off, if you ask me, when this house was a little bit messy."

I couldn't disagree with that. P.J.'s blinds were pulled tightly closed, and a baseball bat was lying beside his bed. I deduced that he was not entirely over his edginess about Lupe's fictional boyfriend.

"So what do you need to talk about?" he asked. "Something on your mind?"

I must be crazy, I thought. I am here to ask P.J. for advice? P.J., whose expertise on boy-girl relationships

128

could be summed up on a 3×5 card with ample room to spare? P.J., who throws wild parties and follows it up by making passes at Lupe? This was my own personal Ann Landers?

"Never mind," I said. I backed hastily out of the room. "I'd better go now."

He looked at me as if convinced I had taken leave of my senses. Maybe I had.

When it came to getting advice, I was between a rock and a hard place. P.J. was hopeless. I could see that now. But Rachel wasn't so hot either. The fact was that Rachel never had gotten over the humiliation of being dumped by Chris after a single disastrous date, and she always put the worst interpretation on everything he did. However, since I urgently needed somebody to talk to, I was in no position to be picky. I ended up going over to Rachel's, after all.

When I went up to her room, Rachel mimed extravagant surprise. "This is some kind of honor! A visit from Andie? It is Andie, isn't it?" She squinted at me. "I seem to remember Andie looked like that."

"Oh, cut it out, Rache." I flopped down at the foot of her bed. Several pounds of magazines and books slid to the floor.

"Sorry," said Rachel. "I realize you've been awfully busy with Chris, whom you are *not* going with."

"Even if I were going with Chris, I don't see why you'd have to get so bent out of shape about it. You told me yourself that you wouldn't touch him with a ten-foot pole."

She sat up. "So *are* you going with him? Honestly,

Andie, you'd better be straight with me. The way it is some kids have come up with the theory that you two are secretly married and that I'm just being a true-blue friend to keep your secret."

I groaned. "Rachel, if I were married, you'd be the first to know. Honestly."

"I wasn't saying I thought it was true. What's the real scoop? Tell me."

I would, I thought. If only I knew what it was myself. How did I really feel about Chris? Did that amazing sense of peace I felt when we kissed mean anything? And if it did, where did I go from there?

Considering I had come to talk, I found myself strangely reluctant to tell Rachel about what had happened. I decided to start with a coldly rational approach to my problem. "There are *so* many reasons why I would not go with Chris," I began. "Millions of reasons." I ticked them off on my fingers. "First of all, I would not want to ruin a beautiful friendship."

"I don't think Chris would let that stop *him,*" put in Rachel.

"Second of all, I just don't want to get involved with somebody. It's not worth it. For a little while you get along, but then you spend the rest of the year picking up the pieces. I'm still reeling from all that junk with Pete."

"Oh, you're over that now," said Rachel brutally. "I noticed it ages ago."

"And, third, if I did want to get involved with somebody, Chris would be my last choice because he's so fickle."

"Yeah," Rachel said, "but don't you sort of figure that with you it'd be different?"

Ouch. Until Rachel said that, I don't think I realized that I had that secret hope. Since she was peering at me as if I were some unusual scientific specimen, I did my best not to look as if she had landed a shot in my heart. I avoided her eyes and checked my nail polish for chips. When at last I figured I could speak without choking, I said, "Everybody thinks they're going to be different, Rachel. I'm too smart to fall into that trap. I don't swallow that romantic garbage. I am one of the extremely few people around here with both feet solidly on the ground." I found my eyes wandering to a large light patch on Rachel's wall. Back when Rachel had had a crush on Chris, she had kept a wall poster there that detailed Chris's complicated love life. Rachel used to say that she had a plan, that she wasn't going to make any of the mistakes his other girls had made. Rachel had thought she was going to be different. Looking at that light patch on her wall, I felt—there was no other word for it—stupid.

Rachel gnawed at a cuticle. She was still watching me curiously. "Just why are you telling me all this, huh?"

She had me there. Why was I telling her this? There had to be some good reason. The actual truth was I had hoped she would help me sort out all my confusion, but it wasn't working out that way. I was only feeling more and more defensive with every word I spoke. "I've been doing some serious thinking," I said finally.

"And you decided you and Chris are just friends and you want to keep it that way, huh?" said Rachel.

"Yes." I felt my face growing warm as I remembered kissing him. I was going to have to be firm in the future, or he might do it again.

"Tell me the truth, Andie. Isn't there any attraction there at all? I'm just curious."

"Well—" I hedged.

"I thought so," said Rachel. She sighed, her worst suspicions confirmed. "So I guess it's just that Chris wants to keep it platonic, huh? It's really best that way. Someday you'll be glad."

"I just told you," I said irritably, "that I had no intention of going with Chris, didn't I?"

She patted my hand, her eyes moist with sympathy.

Eleven

At dinner the next Monday night Mom and Richard announced that P.J. could now have his friends over. He could consider his phone privileges restored, said Richard, and he didn't have to come home directly after school. "We're impressed with how well you've behaved this past month," Richard went on. "And especially with the improvement in those Spanish grades. Now, I expect you to keep an early curfew on the weekends, but except for that, you can go out all you want. Within reason." Richard paused to give P.J. the opportunity to cheer.

"Actually," P.J. said. "I like it fine around here with you guys." He gave a strained smile.

Mom and Richard exchanged puzzled glances. I could see why they couldn't understand his response. I just hoped they didn't start conducting a full-scale investigation of what was behind it.

During the next few days Lupe crept around the house guiltily. I came up behind her one day when she was vacuuming, and she jumped a mile.

"It wouldn't hurt you to give Lupe the occasional *buenos días,*" I told P.J. "I think she's taking it hard that you're not talking to her anymore. She's gotten awfully jumpy. I mean, much worse than usual. You might be a little bit friendly."

He stared at me in amazement. "After the way she sicced that gorilla on me? You must be kidding. I'm not that stupid. Friendly to Lupe!" He snorted. "No, thanks."

It was like that scientific theory we read about in class that explains that a sneeze in China can start a wind that turns into a tornado in Toronto—the effect is not necessarily equal to the cause. I had hoped the threatening letters would make P.J. back off a little, but I never dreamed they would turn him into a recluse and Lupe into a bundle of nerves.

Friday afternoon Lupe started cleaning out the refrigerator. She began by stacking food on the counter. A big bowl of baking soda and soap suds was on the floor at her feet. When I tried to get an apple out of the fridge, she jumped as if I'd hit her with a cattle prod. I smiled in what I hoped was a reassuring manner and wandered into the family room to find P.J.

"I think I might go to the ball game tonight," he said with studied casualness. "I've asked Chris and Dooley. And Rachel is going with us. If you want to come, too, that's fine." P.J. cast a quick glance at the kitchen and Lupe. "Actually, I'd like to be surrounded by a crowd, if you know what I mean."

I was glad Mom had gone out to the library. It meant I could speak freely. "I don't know what you're so upset about, P.J. Those threats are practically ancient history now. You haven't got any more of them, have you?"

"Yeah, but I keep thinking maybe he's just lulling me into a false sense of security."

"I'll go to the ball game with you all. I'll even bring along a roll of nickels so if anybody makes a move toward you, I can knock him out."

"Go, ahead. Laugh. Dooley's not laughing. He thinks I ought to pack a knife. I told him all about it."

"Did you tell Chris too?"

"Sure, but you know Chris. He laughs everything off."

Just then Chris came bounding up the steps from the garage and into the family room.

"Speak of the devil," said P.J. sourly as Chris threw open the door.

"Hi there, sports fans," said Chris. "Got anything to eat around here?"

"Lupe's cleaning the refrigerator," P.J. explained. "You'd better stay out of her way."

"Does she have to do it right now?"

"Everything doesn't wait on your convenience, you know, Hamilton."

I jumped up. "I'll see you guys later."

"Where are you going?" asked Chris.

"Upstairs. I've got a lot to do." Ever since the episode with our kiss, I'd felt uncomfortable around Chris. I could say over and over again that nothing had changed, but still I felt uncomfortable. It was getting harder and harder for me to maintain my usual rational point of view when Chris fixed his baby blues on me.

"Andie said she's going to go to the game with us," said P.J.

"Hey, that's what I was just going to ask her," protested Chris.

"Well, I've already asked her," said P.J. "So would you shut up about it?"

"Just because you're in a foul mood, you don't have to ruin everybody's day," said Chris.

"I'm not in a foul mood. But when a person explains that his life may be in danger and another person laughs in his face, then that first person is bound to have some feelings about it, if you know what I mean."

"I'll see you guys later!" They didn't seem to notice as I slipped away.

I could hear their raised voices as I went upstairs. I'm not sure what obscure impulse made me suddenly sit down on the stairs and listen, but that's what I did. They weren't making any effort to keep their voices down.

"Just what are you telling Andie these days, anyway?" Chris said.

"I don't know what you're talking about."

136

"Ever since you got ungrounded, she's been avoiding me."

"Maybe you ought to check your brand of mouthwash." P.J. snickered.

"Real funny, P.J., real funny. Has Andie said anything to you about me?"

"Jeez, Chris, if she had, you think I'd tell you?"

"If you don't want your teeth rammed down your throat you might," said Chris.

P.J. snorted. "What's this all of a sudden about Andie? I thought it was all settled that she was a civilian. Can't you keep your hands off one single girl in the entire school, huh?"

"Who fixed it so that you get to write the rules?" asked Chris.

"So the answer is no, huh? You can't. You are pathetic, you know that? You ought to get help. I'm not the only one saying it, either. Alana Jackson told me there's a chapter in her psych book that's you to the letter. She's thinking about writing an article on it for the school paper."

"You're somebody to talk," said Chris, stung. "Who is it who hit on your housekeeper? At least I don't pick on somebody who can't afford to tell me to get lost."

"Keep Lupe out of this, you creep. She does speak some English, you know. Can't you see you're making her nervous?"

"Don't worry about it. I'm out of here."

"You don't want to leave a message for Andie?" I suspected P.J. wasn't quite as mad at Chris as he was making out, but Chris was so annoyed he wasn't picking up on it. I heard the door slam behind him.

I got up right away because I didn't want P.J. to catch me sitting on the stairs and listening. The doorbell rang, and after a second's hesitation I trotted downstairs to answer it.

To my surprise, a tall dark man in a blue shirt stood at the front door. His hair was slicked back, and there was a small round Band-Aid on his jaw as if he had cut himself shaving. I glanced behind him but saw no delivery truck, just a plain blue Chevrolet parked next to the curb.

"I'm here to get Lupe," he said.

I was completely rocked by that. "I'm not sure," I stuttered. "She's working." My first incoherent thought was that Chris had hired somebody to impersonate Lupe's boyfriend. My next thought, which was even less lucid, was that Chris's letters had somehow caused our fictional character to materialize. Here was Carlos in living color. His arms hung loosely at his sides, his feet were spread apart, and the whole set of his body seemed to say he was ready to fight. I took a step backward.

"What's the matter, Andie?" P.J. whispered, his voice shaking. He had flattened himself against the foyer wall, hoping, obviously, that Lupe's boyfriend wouldn't see him.

"He says he's come to see Lupe," I said. I eyed the man anxiously. But then decided he must really be a friend of Lupe's or else how would he know where she worked? The puzzling thing to me was that she hadn't come out to greet him. She must have heard his voice.

"Maybe Lupe doesn't want to see him," P.J. whispered.

The guy pushed past me. "Nobody can keep me from seeing my wife," he said.

I ran after him. "Look," I said. "I think you'll have to wait until Lupe gets off work. Uh, sir?"

He strode right past the open door where P.J. was cringing without even glancing at him.

Then I saw Lupe. She was cowering in front of the kitchen sink, clutching a package of frozen spinach to her chest. The stranger let loose with a torrent of angry Spanish. Lupe began answering back very quickly in Spanish.

"She says he's going to kill her," P.J. told me, his eyes widening. He must have tiptoed up behind me while the other two were shouting.

"She's crazy," snarled the man. "A wife's supposed to be with her husband. She's going with me." He strode over and grabbed Lupe by the hand. Lupe promptly sat down on the floor, a dead weight. But to my amazement this didn't stop the guy. He just dragged her a foot or two along the vinyl floor. Lupe shot me an imploring look. *"Me ayuda!"* she cried.

"Hey, wait a minute!" yelled P.J. "You can't just come in here and drag her off like this." P.J. strode toward them. The guy let go of Lupe to sock P.J.— hard. P.J. fell backward. Lupe's husband watched as P.J. sagged against the refrigerator.

The guy's dark hair had fallen into his eyes.

Seeing my chance, I grabbed a kitchen chair and brought it down on his head. He staggered. I guess he hadn't expected me to attack him. Lupe darted up and ran to the family room. P.J. pushed himself up against the refrigerator. While Lupe's husband was still confused, I grabbed the frying pan on the stove and brought it down hard on his head. To my astonishment, he went limp.

"Gosh, I hope I haven't hurt him," I whimpered.

"Crikey," said P.J. "We've got to call the cops, Andie!"

"You don't think I've done him any serious damage, do you?" I asked anxiously.

Chris burst in the kitchen door. "What's going on? I was out in the garage and heard all this noise." He spotted the unconscious body on the kitchen floor, then looked at me with the frying pan still in hand. His mouth fell open.

"I think I'd better call an ambulance," I said.

Chris knelt beside the unconscious man. "He's okay. He's breathing and his color's all right. What happened?"

"I hit him with a frying pan."

"Yeah, but who *is* he?"

P.J. fingered his jaw. "He's Lupe's husband. Jeez, I hope he doesn't come to before the cops get here. Forget the ambulance, Andie. I'm calling nine-one-one." He reached for the phone and began dialing.

"I didn't mean to hit him so hard," I whispered. I

felt definitely weak in the knees. "Chris, I think I'm going to faint."

Chris scooped me up in his arms. "Go ahead and faint," he said. He held me, grinning at me.

I didn't struggle. Maybe, technically, he had swept me off my feet, but I didn't care. It had been a rough afternoon, and I figured I was entitled. Then he kissed me.

"Do you two have to stand there making out at a time like this," complained P.J. "Can you believe there's no answer at nine-one-one? Je-rusalem, if this was supposed to be my lucky year, I hope I don't live to see an unlucky one." He jiggled the receiver.

Mom threw open the kitchen door and looked at us blankly. Chris quietly let me slide down to my feet, his face suddenly expressionless. Lupe ran her hands through her hair and shrieked something in Spanish.

"It's about time!" P.J. yelled into the receiver. "Where've you people been? I want to report an assault, make that two assaults, and an attempted kidnapping!"

"Hi, Mom," I said weakly.

"Andie!" cried Mom. "What's going on? Who is that man?"

I could see why Mom was taken aback. A big frozen turkey, celery, and various miscellaneous foods were strewn all over the kitchen in such quantities that it looked as if the fridge had exploded, and Lupe, who had come back into the kitchen, was doing an imitation of Medea having a very bad day. And then there was the unconscious man on the kitchen floor.

I could hear P.J. giving our address to the 911 operator.

"That's Lupe's husband," I explained. "He tried to take her away, but she didn't want to go. Then P.J. got into it and he socked P.J.—so I hit him with the frying pan."

Lupe wiped her eyes with her apron. She was talking a mile a minute, but I couldn't understand a word of it. Every now and then P.J. stuck in a translation.

"Lupe says she ran away from him because he hit her," P.J. explained.

Mom tut-tutted and put her arm around Lupe protectively.

"Lupe says she's afraid he'll kill her," P.J. went on. "She doesn't know how he found her, and she doesn't want to go home with him."

"Your Spanish has improved remarkably, P.J.," Mom said, staring at him. "Absolutely remarkably."

The doorbell rang. "That must be the cops," said Chris. "I'll get it."

"The cops," said P.J. "The dispatcher must have radioed them."

They arrived just in time. Lupe's husband was beginning to stir and was groaning. I just hoped that all that was wrong with him was a dreadful headache. I had been so scared when I hit him with the frying pan that I had brought it down awfully hard. The two police officers strode into the room.

"Look," said Chris hastily. "I'm not a witness or

anything. I'd better shove off. I'll be back later, Andie. Okay?"

Mom sank weakly into a chair.

"What seems to be the trouble, ma'am?" asked one of them.

"Well—" Mom looked confused. "I had just gone out to the library for a minute, and when I got back—" She made a helpless gesture toward all the food spread all over the kitchen.

Chris came back after supper, as he had promised, and threw a pebble at my bedroom window. I slipped downstairs to talk to him.

"Everybody calmed down?" he asked.

"Not exactly. Richard came home right away, of course. He says the police can't hold Lupe's husband very long, so the big thing is to get Lupe out of town to some unknown destination. Mom and Richard are going to drive her to the bus station as soon as she gets packed. They know some people in Washington she can go to work for."

Chris shook his head wonderingly. "Jeez, didn't you just about die when the guy showed up?"

"For sure." I shivered. "And you know what? I had this creepy feeling that maybe we had made him materialize by writing those letters. It sure explains why Lupe hardly ever went out and why she got so scared when P.J. told her about the letters."

Chris and I sat on the front stoop. No one had remembered to close the blinds of the house, and light was streaming out the windows so I could make out his old cutoffs and red sweatshirt that was so faded it was more of a pink. I felt a rush of warmth toward him. Good old Chris, always there when I needed him.

"I can't believe the way you laid that guy out," Chris said.

"Working out isn't everything, you know," I said smugly. Since I had been assured that Lupe's husband hadn't suffered any permanent damage, I was feeling pretty pleased with the part I had played in subduing him. I had undeniably shown a certain amount of presence of mind. I might just possibly consider a career as a secret agent. Why not? It turned out, somewhat to my surprise, that I was resourceful and cool under fire.

"I hope you aren't going to make a habit of that stuff," said Chris.

"What?" He had interrupted my train of thought. I was already imagining myself getting a meritorious award from Interpol. Maybe a gold medal even.

"I mean you aren't going to go on hitting guys with frying pans when you get ticked off at them, are you?"

"Don't worry." I smiled. "I wouldn't get that ticked off at you."

He put his arm around my waist, and I snuggled comfortably up against him.

"Andie," he said, "I've got something I have to tell you."

I stiffened. Why was Chris suddenly sounding as if

he was about to make a public announcement? I didn't like it.

He coughed uncomfortably. "I think we're going together," he said.

"Where did you get that idea?" I said uneasily. I didn't like the label "going together." I associated it with bad things—nasty scenes, breaking up. Couldn't people be close and warm with each other without "going together"?

Chris gave me a look, and it definitely was not a let's-be-friends look.

I rested my head on his shoulder. "Okay," I said with bad grace. "If you say so, I guess we are going together."

"Well, that's okay, isn't it?"

"I just don't want to be tied down."

"Me, either!" he protested. "I didn't say anything about being tied down, did I?"

"And I hate people getting all possessive and jealous," I went on.

"We are in absolute agreement. Hey, you know the way I feel about that. Look at it this way, Andie— nothing's different from the way it's been. And you said yourself that we had a good thing going."

"It's true." I admitted. "We do have a good thing."

"All right, then."

Then he kissed me. We kissed for a long time. After brief reflection, I decided it was the best forty seconds of my entire life.

"There's just one thing," Chris said, pulling away

from me. "I don't think we'd better push our luck, do you?"

"What?" I shook my head and tried to catch my breath.

"I mean I don't think we'd better tell P.J. that we wrote those letters." He grinned.

I had to agree.

Twelve

Rachel sat hunched forward at my dressing table, her hands between her knees on the bench, her black hair streaming forward over her shoulders. "Okay, tell me again how you could be going with Chris and not know it," she said. "I'm not sure I got it straight."

"I don't know, Rache. It's kinda hard to explain."

"I'll bet! That's because it doesn't make any sense. Not to mention that this is going to be very embarrassing for me at school. I said all that time that you were just friends."

"We *are* friends. It's just that I finally realized that our relationship was not entirely platonic."

"And when was that? At what precise point?"

"It happened sort of by degrees," I said in a muted voice. I could almost hear "Andie and Chris sitting in a tree" and my ears began to feel warm.

"That's okay," Rachel said, hurt. "You don't have

to tell me, if you don't want to. I'm only your best friend."

"It's just hard to explain. I just didn't want to get involved. And knowing Chris the way I did, all those girls of his, his reputation. And then everything I'd been through with Pete, I was kind of in a weird state of mind."

"That's the part I'm clear about," said Rachel. "I've heard all about how you didn't want to get involved. It's the other stuff that's mixing me up. The stuff about how you finally did get involved."

I shifted my position uncomfortably. "We just decided we were more than friends. But Chris and I don't believe in that possessive stuff, that you-belong-to-me-I-belong-to-you stuff. The one thing we absolutely agree on is that we each have to maintain our independence. We just go on the same as usual. That's all there is to it. If people want to call it 'going together,' okay, but we're not getting into all that sick jealousy stuff."

Rachel raised her eyebrows. "So you're saying it's okay with you if Chris sees other girls?"

"The question doesn't arise," I said loftily. "Chris isn't interested in other girls. But if Chris wants to split a pizza with some girl at the mall, or if I go over and do my homework with some guy, neither of us is going to die."

"Do you realize that you are turning slightly green even as we speak?"

"I am not!" I exclaimed indignantly.

"I take that back. I'm sorry I said that." Rachel looked abashed. "That was petty. I think it's really great that you and Chris are getting together. And the thing is, I really think that it may last more than the usual three days. Chris hasn't been out with anybody else for weeks and weeks. The word is that he's truly fixated on you. I mean, this could be love."

"Oh, I don't know," I demurred. "It's certainly something good, anyway."

"No, really. I'm serious. I think it's different from all Chris's other things because you two really like each other." Rachel sighed. "He had to grow up sometime. And you were just the lucky duck who was standing by when he did. That's the way I see it."

I grinned. "Hey, don't flatter me, Rache. It may go to my head."

The doorbell rang downstairs.

I jumped up. "That's Chris. We're going out for burgers."

Rachel followed me downstairs. Chris was standing at the front door, the sun gleaming on his fair hair. "Hi-ya, Rachel. We're going for burgers. Uh, you want to come along?"

"Well, gee, if you insist," she said, beaming. "That would be great."

Chris's eyes met mine in dismay.

Rachel threw her hands up. "Just kidding, you guys."

We smiled a little nervously as we got in the car.

"A day without Rachel," Chris said under his breath, "is like a week in the country."

"Stop it!" I shoved him and we both laughed.

As Chris's car tore down the bluff, the exhaust puffed out behind us like a sigh of relief.

About the Author

JANICE HARRELL decided she wanted to be a writer when she was in the fourth grade. She grew up in Florida and received her master's and doctorate degrees in eighteenth-century English literature from the University of Florida. After teaching college English for a number of years, she began to write full time.

She lives in Rocky Mount, North Carolina, with her husband, a psychologist, and their daughter. Ms. Harrell is a compulsive traveler—some of the countries she has visited are Greece, France, Egypt, Italy, England, and Spain—and she loves taking photographs.

The Linda Stories

*Read all about the boys
in Linda's life...
from her first crush to
the ups and downs of
a powerful true love.*

continued